THE NICK
OF TIME

Also by San Culberson

IN BETWEEN MEN

THE NICK OF TIME

SAN CULBERSON

Kensington Publishing Corp.

http://www.kensingtonbooks.com

DAFINA BOOKS are published by

Kensington Publishing Corp.
850 Third Avenue
New York, NY 10022

All Kensington Titles, Imprints, and Distributed Lines are available at special quantity discounts for bulk purchases for sales promotions, premiums, fund-raising, and educational or institutional use. Special book excerpts or customized printings can also be created to fit specific needs. For details, write or phone the office of the Kensington special sales manager: Kensington Publishing Corp., 850 Third Avenue, New York, NY 10022, Attn: Special Sales Department, Phone: 1-800-221-2647.

Dafina and the Dafina logo Reg. U.S. Pat. & TM Off.

ISBN-13: 978-0-7582-1521-5
ISBN-10: 0-7582-1521-5

First trade paperback printing: December 2006
First mass market printing: November 2008

10 9 8 7 6 5 4 3 2 1

Printed in the United States of America

Girlfriend,

as you know,

I've been through a lot of shit this year.

But I'm writing to tell you the end is here.

The divorce is final and that man is gone.

So now it's time for me to get my party on!

Thursday at Ray's, at a quarter past 7.

Plan to be there until way past 11.

Food and drink…everything's on me…

It's all to celebrate the fact that I'm free!

CHAPTER 1

The invitation was a little bold, I admit, but it was the start of a new beginning for me, a new life, like my girl Patti sang, *"A New Attitude!"* I was 29 years old and newly divorced. *Played* and put off by a man who had stood with me before God and my family not six years before and promised to love, cherish, and honor me. . . .

This may be a little off the subject, but I think the grooms are not really grasping the *true* meaning of the marriage vows. It may prove beneficial to all interested parties if the wording was a tad more specific; something like, "Do you promise to bring your paycheck home? Do you promise to consult me before you spend $400 on DVDs at Best Buy? Do you promise to at least try and wash your ass properly?" And most importantly, "Do you promise to fuck me and only me for as long as we both shall live?" I'm just saying a little clarity would be nice.

So *anyway*, I decided that I was not going to let one big *D* adjective (Divorced) allow a lot of other little *d* adjectives to define me. Words like "disheartened," "disillusioned," "down," "dirty," "destructive" . . . you get my drift. I *refused* to be those things.

I knew the papers were coming—the final divorce papers. I thought I was ready for them, so I was surprised at the lump that had worked its way to my throat when I opened the envelope. I sat on the edge of my bed for a long time that evening, holding the papers and thinking about Fiona and Wilson Lawson (me and my ex), the way we used to be. By the way, in the future, he (Wilson) will only be referred to as *my ex-hole* (a combination of ex-husband and asshole). I made that word up, and I'm really thinking about contacting Webster's to find out how I can get it included in their next dictionary.

Like I said, I sat there for what seemed like hours reminiscing about the way we were; then suddenly, I remembered how that asshole looked me straight in the eye not two days before I found out for real that he was fucking that *whore*, excuse me, that *woman* . . . no, actually, *ho* is a more accurate description.

Time out. In case you haven't noticed, some aspects of my marriage and divorce continue to be a sore spot, so I'm going to do us all a favor and get some things off my chest so that I can get on with it.

First of all, every woman knows that one of the easiest things to have *in this world* is another woman's man (at least temporarily), and one of the hardest things is to make it work with your own man once the first petal has fallen off of the rose. Therefore, I can only conclude that she is a lazy bitch and that my asshole ex-husband is easily had. I'm through. That's all I have to say about them. I have better things to talk about.

On with the story. I stood up from the bed, went to the mirror, and thought about the good in my life. What I concluded was this: I still had my good looks (Angela Bassett arms and a Halle Barry waistline), my law degree, an excellent chance for advancement at the law firm that I had been with for two years, money in the bank, a new condo in Case City right outside of Durham, my good health, and friends and family who loved me to no end. I had more than one reason to have a party.

With the help of my best girlfriend, Nicole, I planned the party in twelve days. We found the spot, hired a caterer, and invited the twenty-six most fabulous women that we knew. Nicole and I had been friends since before we stopped playing hopscotch, and during the past year she had kept me from doing all kinds of crazy shit.

The day before the party my mom called my office and asked me to stop by after work. She told me that my sister had told her about "some party" that I was having. There was a question in her voice that I didn't want to answer. I *knew* I shouldn't have invited Ramona. Remember I said that we invited the twenty-six most fabulous women that we knew . . . Well, my sister was number 27. She had moved back to Durham only five months before.

We didn't have anything in common except our parents and our failed marriages. But I *had* to invite her because she was my sister. I don't know what Ramona had said to my mother, but whatever it was, I could tell by the tone in my mother's voice that she had some advice for me.

Dutiful daughter that I am, I got to my parents house around seven o'clock, even though I was drop-dead tired. My mother opened the door for me and pulled me into the hallway. She looked me up and down before speaking, "I made a cake for your party, carrot, your favorite, though I don't know why a bunch of women would get together and have a *party* because your marriage failed. I hope these women are not a bunch of bull daggers." She said what she had to say with an even mixture of concern and disgust.

I followed her to the kitchen at the back of the house and sat down at the table. I was not offended. I was amused. There are two inarguable facts about my mother: one, she's beautiful, and two, she's a *loony toon*. The first has undoubtedly kept my father from having her committed at some point during their thirty-six-year marriage.

"Well . . . ?"

"Well what?" I asked her.

"*Are they bulldaggers?*"

"Mom, I believe the more appropriate term is *lesbian*. And to answer your question, I *assume* that they're mostly heterosexual women, but I couldn't swear to it in court. Thanks for asking." I looked appreciatively at the two cakes on the counter. Another thing that had probably kept my father from committing her was his sweet tooth. My mother's carrot cake was so good that it was almost otherworldly.

My mother took milk from the refrigerator and poured a glass. She cut into one of the cakes and placed the slice and the glass of milk in front of me. I smiled at her thankfully, cut into the cake with my fork, and waited for her to continue. She sat across from me and fixed a look of motherly concern on her face.

"Baby, I know this thing with Wilson has twisted you all around inside, but you need to be careful." I didn't have to say anything. I knew she would elaborate. "You have to watch out for those bull . . . *lesbians*. And don't go turning into one of those man-hatin' women. A woman needs a man. I know you young girls think all you need is a pocketful of money and one of those vibrators, but you can get hooked on those things." She whispered the last part.

"*What?*" It was my policy not to ask my mother questions when she was giving advice, but she caught me off guard.

"You can get hooked on those things . . . your sister did."

"Mom, how would you know that?" I had to ask.

"Well, remember when I went to visit your sister in Atlanta after her and Pierce got divorced? She had one of those vibrators sitting up on the couch. It was a big green one. She introduced it to me; she was calling it Derrick. Saying she was going to have 'him' fitted for a custom suit so he could start going with her to social functions.

"Before I went to sleep that night she apologized because he didn't speak to me. She said he had laryngitis. I think she brought that thing back to Carolina with her. You know she hasn't had a date in three years." She stood up from the table and patted me on the back.

"All I'm saying is, get you some *real* dick, honey."

Like I said, my mom is crazy . . . crazy like a *fox.* I kissed her smooth brown cheek without comment. I knew from experience that one sarcastic comment from me and I could kiss my carrot cake good-bye. I took my empty plate to the sink and picked up the uncut cake.

"It's not enough cake to share with everyone at the party so I'll probably just take it to work with me tomorrow and share with some of the other associates." She walked me back to the front door where I kissed her again. "Tell Dad I said hi."

"*Think about what I said!*" I heard her shout out just as I was pulling away from the curb.

CHAPTER 2

I felt it was imperative that I look like a million dollars at my divorce celebration. Therefore, I am pleased to report that when I walked into Ray's that night the door man wouldn't take my money, the dj stopped the music when he saw me, mouths fell open as I walked by, and I got four indecent proposals and two marriage proposals before I made it to the room where my party was being held. Okay, that didn't really happen . . . but the doorman *did* let me in at no charge (something about it being ladies' night), and I looked damned good!

Nicole was in the private room giving last-minute instructions to the *female* bartender—we had decided that it would be best not to invite any men to the party, because at some point there was bound to be some male bashing (good-natured, of course). I walked to the free-standing bar in the back corner of the room and greeted my friend with a hug. She hugged me back tight and handed me the glass of champagne that she had waiting for me.

"You look good," she told me as I took a sip from the glass. I twirled around in my knee-length red jersey dress, pulled the thigh-high split to the side, and positioned my size eight—okay, size nine—silver sandal so that she could pay proper homage to my entire ensemble. She laughed and grabbed me so fast for another hug that I almost spilled my champagne. "I take that back, you look *great.*"

"So do you." Nicole and I could have been sisters except we had different parents and our looks were totally opposite. Nicole was about five feet tall and had been blessed/cursed with a Betty Boop body. She wore her naturally curly hair cropped close to her head, and dimples were on each of her golden brown cheeks.

I'm five eight, have skin the color of 2% chocolate milk like my mama, honey-colored eyes like my daddy, and a thing about getting my hair cut like my grandmother. I usually wore my hair in some sort of sophisticated updo, but for the occasion of my coming out party, I let the black curls hang past my shoulders. Nicole and I didn't *look* like sisters, but as far as I was concerned, we were.

"I want you to look at the buffet." She motioned for the bartender to top off my champagne before I followed her to the buffet. It was perfect—fruit, cheese, vegetables, dips, and crackers. I lifted the lid of a beautiful sterling chafing dish to discover shrimp etouffee (one of my favorites); another chafing dish was filled with chicken breast and vegetables in a delicious-smelling cream sauce. Soft-looking rolls were piled high in a straw bread basket.

"Everything looks great, Nicole."

"Check out the cake." She gestured to a small table at the very end of the buffet. On it was an elaborate pink and white cake with GIRLS RULE . . . BOYS DROOL written in fancy script in the center of the cake. The childish truism made me smile. I turned to my friend again and was surprised to feel tears gathering in the corners of my eyes.

She took both of my hands in hers and smiled brightly at me. "I know, I know."

"I *know* you know, but I'm going to say it *anyway*. You've been such a blessing to me during the last year. I don't know what I would have done without your support. You have single handedly kept ex-hole out of a casket and me out of prison." She laughed like she was supposed to, but I was serious.

"I think you've spent more time with me this last year than you have with Anderson. When you get home tonight, tell your husband that I am officially giving him his wife back." I looked around the room again, then back at Nicole with gratitude. "And helping me throw this party together on such short notice . . . What can I say? I love you, girl."

"I love you, too, Fiona. You know you're my sister."

A tear spilled down her cheek and got caught in one of her dimples. I started to go ahead and give in and let my emotion flow down my cheeks, but my foundation cost $45 a bottle, and *hello,* we were having *a* party. "Suck it up," I told her, "my first guest has arrived."

A couple of hours later, the twenty-six most fabulous women that we knew, several that we *didn't* know, *and* my sister were feeling "nothing else to drink for me because I have to drive home tonight" mellow. *I* was feeling "not only will I not be driving tonight, I won't be going into my office tomorrow morning, so I can drink whatever the hell I want" mellow. We were all having a great time. The buffet was almost down to the bare bones, but the cake was still intact, waiting patiently for someone to cut into it.

A couple of women, Renessa from law school and Toni, my best office buddy, had expressed their condolences to me because of the sudden death of my marriage. I informed them without missing a beat that the party was a celebration and condolences were out of order. My sister was sitting in a corner talking to a woman we had grown up with. Her name was Beverly, and Ramona *knew* that I didn't like her, which was probably why she had invited her to my party. The fact that my sister doesn't like me is not at all worrisome to me, because the truth is, she doesn't like anyone.

I didn't like Beverly because she had stolen my first boyfriend. Well, Terry wasn't exactly my *first* boyfriend, but he was the first boy who I had seriously considered having sex with. I guess I considered too long, because before I could say "yeah" or "nay," Beverly just stepped up to the plate—or to be more accurate, the north side of our high school building—and gave him what he had been begging me for.

I took the last sip from the champagne flute that I was holding and stared at Beverly long and hard. It seemed to me that sisters had been interfering with my love life since before I really had one. I went to the bar for a refill before I allowed my somber thoughts to clear my head. I was swaying to the beat of the music and enjoying watching my friends enjoying themselves when I noticed Nicole making her way to the center of the room.

She lifted her glass up and tapped on it with a fork that she had removed from the buffet. "May I have your attention, ladies?" When she didn't get everyone's attention, she repeated the words a little louder. "Ladies, please, your attention." When nearly everyone was quiet and most eyes were focused on her, she started to speak.

"As you know, we have all gathered here at the request of our friend, our *dear* friend Fiona." The waitress or *someone* filled my glass again without being asked. I continued to sip (gulp, if you want to know the *real* truth) the sweet champagne as I looked toward Nicole with anticipation and amusement. Even in the dimly lit room I could see that she was up to something.

"Fiona is newly divorced. It is a widely publicized fact that Fiona's husband was screwing around. Don't pretend to be surprised, ladies, they all do it at some point. Well, not *my* husband." Everyone in the room laughed at her exaggerated denial. "But then Fiona doesn't know how to please a man like I do." Everyone laughed harder at the joke, including me . . . because believe me, it *was* a joke.

"Some of us feel that Fiona should have known a long time before she actually *admitted it to herself* that Wilson was cheating on her. Right now, ladies, we will review the goings-on the last few months of her marriage in something we will call 'Fiona, you should have known he was cheating when . . .'" Nicole took a good look at me before continuing. I could tell she was trying to make sure that I was okay with her little game. I was, so I smiled into my glass and nodded my head for her to go on.

"I'll start and then I'll open the floor to you, ladies." She cleared her throat dramatically to signify the start of the game. She shook her head, feigning sadness. "Fiona, you should have known he was cheating when he came back from his fraternity reunion and you found condoms in his luggage. He told you that the condoms weren't for him, but for the brothers who didn't practice safe sex. Whenever he saw one of them going off with some skeezer, he would offer them one. When he offered you up that bullshit, you should have *known* he was cheating."

There was more laughter in the room before Lenny, another long-term friend, spoke up. "You should have known he was cheating when you woke up one night and discovered him having phone sex in the kitchen." The laugher continued as more women said their two cents' worth.

"You should have known he was cheating when you found that black bra and panty set in his briefcase and he told you he didn't know how it got there."

"You should have known he was cheating when you found a receipt in his pocket showing that he had bought women's underwear on his credit card and he told you that his secretary had started her period at work and he let her use his credit card to buy what she needed instead of letting her go home." The "should have known's" got more outrageous. And I was laughing so hard that tears were running down my cheeks.

"You should have known he was cheating when his secretary called you at *home* and said, 'Are you stupid, bitch? I'm fucking yo' husband.'"

"You should have really known he was cheating when you received a certified package in the mail from the secretary. The note said, *Enclosed you will find a picture of me fucking yo' husband*, and the picture *was* of her fucking *yo'* husband!"

"You should have known he was cheating on you when you asked him, and he said, 'Baby, I would never cheat on you.'"

"You finally did know he was cheating when you walked into his office and said, 'What the hell are you two doing?' and the secretary looked up and said, 'We're screwing, what does it look like?'" It took about ten to fifteen minutes for everyone who had something to say to say it. I don't know if it had something to do with the unusually large volume of champagne that I had consumed, but that shit was funny to me. Not all of it had actually happened, but enough of it had happened to prove the saying "Hindsight is 20/20." I was not the only one in the room doubled over with laughter.

After the last "You should have known," Nicole brought the focus back to her. "You know we love you, girl." She wiped tears of laughter from her eyes before continuing. She held out her hand for me to join her in the center of the room. When I was able to get myself together I did.

"Fiona, you've been through a lot these last several months, and you have handled yourself with grace. In other words, you've kept it together. You've kept your sense of humor, your figure, and your sanity. I hope that if I am ever in a similar situation that I can pull off a *Fiona*." We hugged each other tight, like the sisters that we were. When we let each other go, she reached over and took a red basket from a nearby table.

"We have a surprise for you. Since this is the start of your new and lucky life, we bought you some lottery tickets." And one by one the ladies in the room came to the center and dropped their tickets into the basket. It was like the way some offerings were orchestrated in the Baptist church. Every one of the ladies gave me a hug, and several whispered words of encouragement in my ear. It felt wonderful to be on the receiving end of so much love.

I noticed at that point that a couple of men were disassembling the buffet, and that my sister, Ramona, had not thrown a lottery ticket into the basket, nor had she given me a hug. I clapped my hands gleefully when Nicole handed me the basket. I shouted out a general thank you to everyone in the room. It was getting late, so some of my guests started to leave. I went for a refill again and Nicole followed me.

"I can see I'm going to have to drive you home."

"No, you don't; I'm calling a cab. I'll get my car in the morning."

"But what if someone breaks in?"

Before I could respond, Ramona walked up to say her good-byes. My sister was an attractive woman; at one point she had been very attractive, but since her divorce her expression had remained perfectly sour.

"I'm out of here, Fee. I rode with Beverly and she's ready to go." She didn't try to hug me.

"Ramona, Fee is taking a cab home . . . can you drive her truck to your house and let her pick it up tomorrow? I don't want her to leave it here overnight." From my champagne haze I saw that Ramona's face became more sour.

"I don't like to drive other people's cars."

"She's your *sister,* for God's sake."

Ramona rolled her eyes at Nicole and squinted her eyes at me as she spoke. "So long as you know that if something happens to your truck while it's in my possession I'm not responsible." I smiled and let the champagne continue to work its magic. Ramona snapped at me when I didn't say anything. "Well, give me the keys." I fumbled in my small Louis Vuitton bag for the keys to my new BMW X5. When I found them, I took my door key from the ring and dropped it back into my bag.

"Hurry up, Fee, I have somebody waiting for me at home."

Nicole looked at her in disbelief. "You're *seeing* someone, Ramona?"

My sister snatched the keys out of my hand before responding to Nicole's question. "As a matter of fact, I am. His name is Derrick and he's *very* good to me." I almost choked on the hard laughter that bubbled up in my throat. Ramona narrowed her eyes suspiciously. "Is there something funny, Fee?"

"No, I'm happy for you, Ramona. I'll have to have the two of you for dinner."

"Don't bother, and don't bother calling me to pick you up for work tomorrow. You can pick your car up after six. And happy divorce." She adjusted her black top and went over to where Beverly was standing, presumably to tell her that she wouldn't be riding home with her." Nicole and I watched her black slacks move across the room.

"Your sister is something else. I can't believe she found a man who's willing to put up with her attitude." My laugh was more like a giggle. I was really feeling the champagne by then. The bubbles were tickling my insides and I didn't care that I had a silly grin on my face.

"*You are so drunk.* I'm going to take these lottery tickets home with me. . . . You'd probably leave the winning ticket in the cab." She wrapped her arm around my waist and led me to the other end of the room. "I have something else for you." People continued to break down the buffet, and while most of my guests were leaving, others continued to sit or stand around and talk.

I was tipsy *not* drunk, so I noticed everything around me. I didn't complain about the fact that there were men at my "all-girl party" because both of the men working in the room had strong-looking asses. Nothing like champagne and a divorce to make a girl appreciate a nice ass.

"I'm not drunk." My protest was rather loud even to my own ears. Nicole laughed and handed me a black T-shirt that said DELICIOUSLY DIVORCED. The letters were outlined with sequins, and the neckline was made to look like it had been torn.

"You like?"

"I like." Some women standing close to us admired my new T-shirt. Another couple of my friends left the room after waving in my direction. I thanked Nicole for the shirt and said something about wearing it under all of my business suits.

She asked me if I wanted a slice of the cake that was now circulating, and I told her no because, suddenly, the notion to address my remaining guests struck me.

I started tapping on the champagne glass that I was still holding to get everyone's attention as Nicole had done earlier. I, however, took it a step further and hoisted myself onto one of the tables in the room. At the time, I thought my speech was of presidential quality.

"I want to thank you, ladies, for showing up tonight. I hope you all had a great time, I did." I lifted my flute up to prove my point. "Thank you for the lottery tickets . . . If I win, don't expect a *damn* thing." I may have said *thang*, but I'm not sure. "We gathered here tonight to celebrate my divorce. I know a lot of you ladies are married, and I admire the commitment it takes to put up with so much bullshit! I'm here to tell you that I put up with enough bullshit during the last fifteen months to last me for the rest of my life. I've done my time, ladies; from this day forward I am a certified DFL—*divorcée for life,* baby—and *as God is my witness, I'll never be married again!"* I did my best impression of Scarlett O'Hara, and it would have worked except that when I flung my hand to my forehead (the universal symbol of a Southern woman in distress), my champagne flute flew across the room and crashed.

The noise startled me and I lost my balance on the table. I would have fallen ass first on the hard floor, except that the finest man I had ever seen broke my fall (I swear to God, he was the *finest* man I had ever seen!). I did break the heel off of one of my $350 Jimmy Choo sandals.

I didn't normally spend so much on shoes, but they went with my dress perfectly. Besides, if a girl was going to start a new life, she needed to have the right footwear. Damn, I loved those sandals.

Anyway, I didn't know where he came from, but he caught me as I fell backward off the table. Everyone at the party rushed over asking if I was okay. I didn't respond, not because I was hurt, but because I was busy looking into chocolate brown eyes and steadying myself on a rock-hard chest. He was about 6'1" or 6'2", he looked to be in his mid-to-late thirties, and his skin was a golden syrupy color. The absolute best thing about his looks was the gray streak that started at his temple; I couldn't see where it ended, but I knew immediately that I *had* to find out.

"Are you hurt?" His voice sounded the way I imagine cinnamon would if it had a sound—husky, sweet, and rich. I turned around in his arms and placed my hands on his chest, *to steady myself.* I tried to make my smile as warm as his voice.

"Yes, I am, thanks to you. I hope I didn't hurt *you.*"

"No, you didn't, but looks like your sandal may need a trip to the emergency room." I was about to make some witty remark when Nicole got to us.

"When you start falling off the tables it's time for you to go home, Fee. In fact, it was time for you to go home when you climbed *on* the table." I slid my hands down *his* chest and turned to my friend.

"I'll be leaving in a minute; I'm okay thanks to this big, strong gentleman." I was still pretending to be Scarlett O'Hara. I knew he noticed how I slid my hand down his chest from the way he raised his eyebrows. Nicole noticed too, and she shot me a look, *the look.* I ignored her and put both hands on my hips and tilted my head like we women do when we're trying to be cute.

"I may just owe you my life. Is there anything I can do to repay you?" He was smiling at me, looking me up and down like a man was supposed to do when a woman struck "the pose," but *playa hata* Nicole refused to leave. She took one of my arms and smiled apologetically at my rescuer.

"She's drunk. I'm putting her in a cab." To emphasize her point, she turned me around to face the exit. "Thanks again." I didn't get to see his expression before she pushed me through the door that led to the larger part of the club. I was limping because one heel was on and one was gone.

"Why did you tell him that? I'm not drunk! I was trying to have a conversation."

"Well, you were acting like you were trying to get into his pants."

"And if I was? I'm over twenty-one and *single*, in case you forgot the reason for our celebration tonight."

"Yeah, and you don't want to be over twenty-one, single, and HIV-positive." Nicole Elizabeth Jordan social worker/hypochondriac was always talking about HIV . . . or colon cancer . . . or warts . . . anything remotely medical. I smiled blindly at my three or four remaining guests as she continued to usher me through the room. When we got outside there was a cab waiting by the front entrance.

"How did this cab get here?" I asked.

"The funny thing about cab drivers is they usually come when you call them. That's what they do for a living."

"Very funny, smart ass, but that's not what I meant." I was about to explain what I meant, but I forgot.

She opened the back door of the cab and gave me a quick hug and a kiss on the cheek. "Did you have a good time tonight?" I pushed the hair out of my face and nodded. "Good. Now get in and go home. I'll bring the lottery tickets by some time tomorrow." She closed the door and walked to the driver's side of the cab. She gave the cab driver my address and handed him a twenty. She waved at me as the cab drove off.

I sat back in the seat with my bottom lip slightly poked out. I wasn't ready to go home. I wanted to continue the conversation that I had started with maple syrup man. I had every intention of doing so, but I needed Nicole gone!

When the cabby turned on to the street, I leaned over his shoulder and told him to drive around the block for a few minutes, then circle back and let me out. He looked a little confused until I took a ten out of my purse and tossed it on the seat next to him to go with the twenty he already had. He was more than happy to follow my instructions. I half-formulated a plan as I waited in the back of the cab until I was sure that Nicole was on her way home.

I snuck back into the club like I was a teen-ager sneaking into her parents' house after being out way past curfew. I looked around the front for familiar faces and let out a sigh of relief when I didn't see any. I bent down and slipped my sandals off, then walked confidently through the doors of the party room I had left moments earlier.

CHAPTER 3

Maple syrup man was still there. There was a younger looking man with him who was about to take the last chafing dish out of the room. He stopped wiping the table when he noticed that I was back. His smile was warm and polite.

"Did you forget something?" I looked around the room, then pretended to concentrate on the floor.

"As a matter of fact, I did. Did you notice where the heel of my sandal landed? I was holding both sandals in my hand. I lifted them for him to see. "I was thinking I could probably have it repaired." His look was apologetic as he walked toward the large trash bin in one corner of the room. He reached in and pulled out the silver heel. The wood floor felt cool under my bare feet as I made my way over to him.

"I'm sorry. The way your friend hustled you out of here I thought you were long gone." He held on to the heel a minute longer and pretended to dust it off before handing it to me."

"I'm out. Do you need anything else?" The younger man stuck his head through the door to ask the question.

"No, I'll get the rest." The man nodded his head at me and left the room again. We turned our full attention back to each other. I was smiling at him, he was smiling at me; things were going just like I thought they would when I had decided in the cab to take my mother's advice and get some "real dick".

Yes, that is my plan: real dick real quick! And I will not be judged! I hadn't been involved with anyone—not even a kiss or conversation over a sandwich—since I was first separated. I was ready! And maple syrup man looked as if he was interested.

"That was some party you had. A divorce is the last thing that most women I've encountered would like to celebrate."

"I'm not like most women that you've encountered."

"How do you know that?"

"I know because I'm *totally* unique. There *is* no other woman like me."

"I like that." His looked me up and down, and his tongue moved across his lips. "I like that a lot."

"Anyway . . ." The tension was building a little too fast. My plan was only half formed. I still hadn't figured out how I was going to broach the subject of a one-night stand. "How do you know what I was celebrating? The party was supposed to be strictly *women only.*"

"Well . . ." He held up the wet towel that he

was still holding. "I'm here because I'm part of the cleanup crew. I couldn't help but overhear some of the conversations going on around the room." He finished wiping the table. "By the way, you're much too beautiful to be divorced." I sat at one of the now-empty tables while he completed his work.

"So you think I'm beautiful, do you?" I crossed my legs high, and my dress slid up exposing most of my thighs. *Hey, I am working under time constraints. His job is almost done! It is now or never!*

"Yes, I do." His eyes lingered on my thighs as I had intended.

"I think you're beautiful, too," I said. He laughed at that.

"Thank you . . . *I think.* I don't believe anyone has ever called me beautiful."

"I'm surprised, because you certainly *are* beautiful . . . in a handsome, very manly way of course."

He looked at me doubtfully; then I watched his eyes scan the room as if he was looking for something. He nodded his head slightly, obviously satisfied with his work. He grabbed a box filled with linens from the buffet, then looked back at me.

"I'm done here. Can I walk you to your car?"

"My car is not here. I'm going to have to call a cab." I sighed as if that was the last thing I wanted to do.

"Well then, can I give you a lift somewhere? I promise I won't hurt you." His look was a challenge. I stood up slowly and smoothed my dress over my hips. I think I brushed my tongue across my lips before answering him honestly.

"I thought you'd never ask."

* * *

He made small talk during the fifteen-minute drive to my condo. He was divorced from his wife, had two kids, and had lived in Durham all of his life . . . blah blah blah blah. I didn't talk too much about myself; I didn't see the point. I had never had a one-night stand, but from everything that I had heard or read about them, I was sure that his conversation was way outside the boundaries of one-night stand etiquette.

What was the point of revealing so much about yourself to someone you would never see again? I made up for his gaucheness by ignoring virtually everything he said and concentrating instead on the movement of his full, sexy lips.

A dimple showed in his right cheek when he smiled at a joke that he made. I didn't hear what he said, but I laughed politely and took the opportunity to place my hand on the thigh closest to me. He took his eye off the road for a minute to look at my deliberately placed hand.

"Be careful, you wouldn't want me to get the wrong idea."

"Are you sure about that?" I moved my hand up a little higher on his thigh. He ignored my question and turned his attention back to the road.

"Make a left here." I leaned into him and pointed with my free hand. He turned onto the beautifully landscaped street and I watched the strong cords flex in his hands as he did so. "I'm the last unit on the right." My heart was starting to beat faster; I didn't know if I actually had the courage to proposition him straight out. The buzz from the champagne was wearing off and reality was beginning to set in.

I was sitting in some sort of catering van in front of my house planning to seduce—okay, to *screw*—a man I had never met before. The only thing that kept me from jumping out of the van and running full speed into my house was the fact that the muscles in his thigh felt so damn good under my hand and that I hadn't been that close to a *real* dick in over a year.

He pulled close to the curb but left the engine on. "Would you like to come in?" I massaged the muscles in his thigh lightly, encouraging him to say yes. He didn't take me up on my offer immediately.

"The lady back at the club said that you were drunk . . . are you?"

"Would it matter if I was?" He looked me up and down. His eyes lingered on my thighs, then briefly on my breasts.

"You don't seem drunk to me." We both laughed. I stopped laughing long enough to move my hand up a little higher on his thigh.

"I know exactly what I'm doing." He put the van in Park and turned off the ignition.

"Then lead the way." We both got out, and he followed my swaying hips into the condo. I normally entered through the garage, but I took my key from my bag and let us in the front door. I turned on the light and threw the key and bag on the table in the entrance. The key landed on the floor, but I didn't bother to pick it up. I turned around to face him so quickly that he almost bumped into me. As it was, I could feel the heat from his body.

"What would you like to drink?"

"That depends on how long I can stay." I

leaned in close enough to make his lips part in anticipation.

"Double vodka straight up okay with you?" I whispered. A "you got me" smile spread across his face.

"I'll take scotch on the rocks if you have it."

"I have it. Sit down while I get your drink." I pointed to the chocolate suede sofa in the center of the room. I dropped the broken sandal that I had been holding to the floor and walked to the liquor cabinet. My hips had a little extra sway in them just in case he was watching.

"I like your place."

"Thank you." I had spent more than I probably should have on furniture to make a home that was a reflection of me and *only* me. What I ended up with was a collection of modern and classic furniture in deep earth tones and creamy neutrals.

"Is this Heywood-Wakefield?" I was startled; first, because he recognized my vintage buffet turned liquor cabinet, and second, because instead of sitting on the sofa as I had directed, he had moved silently behind me. His lips were practically touching the back of my head.

"Yeah, it is. The dining room is also." I turned and handed him his drink. He took it and used his free hand to caress the smooth surface of the mellow wood.

"It's beautiful. You a collector?" I smiled at him and nodded my head.

"I have a few pieces." I shrugged my shoulders to let him know it was no big deal, *though it was.* Normally, I would have gone into more detail. I loved my furniture, but I didn't want to make small talk. We stared at each other for a long while, one waiting for the other to make a move or to say something.

He looked me up and down, and when his eyes met mine I didn't turn away.

Apparently, he was tired of skirting the issue directly in front of him—me—because his next words were very much to the point. "I don't really want this drink, what I *want* is for you to take me to your bedroom." No more small talk from maple syrup man.

I felt a thumping at the center of my body; actually, the thumping was down *a little farther*. It was time to separate the woman from the girl. I took the drink from his hand and placed it behind me without looking; I thought about getting a coaster but decided it would mess with the flow of the moment. "Kiss me first," I demanded, and closed my eyes and lifted my face as he moved even closer to me.

He took my face in his hand, and instead of kissing my lips as *I* was anticipating, he brushed his tongue slowly across my forehead. The thumping became a shiver. I felt smooth lips on my eyelids and across my cheeks. His tongue moved lightly down the center of my nose before he pushed it firmly between my lips.

I heard myself moaning as his tongue moved alongside mine. He caught my hair in his hands and pulled me deeper into the kiss. I wanted to move my body closer, but there was no more room between us. The kiss was absolutely *delicious*. His hands massaged my scalp, intensifying the feelings that were building in me. I couldn't touch him because my arms were frozen at my sides.

When he ended the kiss and moved back slightly to look at me I didn't say anything, but I was thinking, Oh my God! He smiled at me and moved his hands to my hips. "That was a good idea. Now take me to your bedroom."

He followed me to my bedroom, and I didn't care about the unmade bed or the discarded outfits on the floor. I stood in front of him unsure about what to do. I knew what we were *going* to do, but I was unsure about how to get the *real* stuff going; fortunately for both of us, *he* wasn't.

He bent his head slightly and slid his hands through the slit in my dress and up to the narrow string on the side of my thong panties. He pulled the little bit of silk down my thighs with confidence. I helped him out by lifting my feet slightly and kicking the panties away from us.

He laughed and I looked down to see what at. "Great aim." I followed his eyes to where my panties had landed on the bedpost. "I bet you throw a mean horseshoe." I was amused myself, a little embarrassed, but amused. Well, to be totally honest, I wasn't embarrassed or amused . . . I was incredibly horny.

"I haven't done it in a while, but I'm sure I could if I had to." I responded to his remark about the horseshoe.

"What do you mean by 'it'?" He had started running his fingers lightly across my butt and thighs.

"I mean it's been a long time since I've thrown a horseshoe."

"Is 'throwing a horseshoe' a euphemism for sex?" The lighting was dim in the room, but I saw the teasing light in his eye.

"Not in my universe." I put my hands on the side of his face and tried to move his lips back to mine, but he wouldn't let me.

"How long has it been since you've made love?" The sound of his voice appealed to me, but I wanted all conversation to cease.

"It doesn't matter how long it's been . . . all that matters is that I'm ready right now." I looked him in the eye, and this time he didn't resist when I pulled his face into mine for another kiss. As we kissed I felt him backing me up toward the bed. When my calves bumped the side rail I broke the kiss and sat down. He stood over me and pulled the dress that was resting around my waist over my head. I reached behind me to un-hook my bra, but he stopped me.

"Let me do that." He moved my hands and uncovered my breast. The bra joined the panties on the bedpost. His eyes lingered on my body for a long time. My shoulders, the breast that he had just exposed, my stomach . . .

He parted my thighs to get a closer look at what was hidden between them before he looked back at me.

"You're beautiful." Okay, a little conversation wasn't so bad.

"Thank you." I took advantage of his position and started to unbutton his shirt. My fingers got tangled in the lush hairs that covered his pecks and tapered down toward his navel. His shoulders were so broad and so hard, I insisted on seeing the rest of him. "No fair, you still have all of your clothes on and I am completely *exposed*." I pressed on his shoulders, urging him to stand up and join me in the buff. He stood up and took off his shirt.

I held my breath when he started to unbuckle his belt. *Anticipaaaation*. It had been a year for me, and I was hoping for something . . . special. When his pants dropped to the floor I sighed and my lips turned up into a smile. JACKPOT! He moved closer to me and I put my hand out to stroke the object of my admiration.

"Nice dick. I hope you know how to use it." I also hoped that my words were a challenge to him. He laughed and pulled me from the bed so that our bodies melted together.

"I think I have the hang of it. I'm guessing I could probably make you cry."

"You could try." I turned my head to the side to let him nibble on my neck.

"I'm also guessing that I'm not going to have to work too hard." One of his hands stroked the wetness between my legs. He probed with one finger and then two. A moan escaped me and I let my head fall on his chest. "Not too hard at all."

I moved away from him, reluctantly, and took the silver box from my nightstand that held condoms and some other things that a single woman should have on hand. I thought it would be kinda sexy to open the condom and put it on him with my mouth like I had seen a woman do in a movie once, but I had never done that before and I didn't want to embarrass myself.

I tossed the condom on the bed and stood behind him, kissing his back and massaging his shoulders as he put it on. When he was done, he grabbed my arms and pulled me in front of him. He kissed me on the side of my face before taking my face in his hands. "If there's anything in particular I need to do to please you, tell me. And when we get to the point where you become speechless . . . *and you will* . . . just guide me." We laughed together as we fell back onto the bed and into each other.

He didn't make me cry, but he *did* make my eyes water.

CHAPTER 4

I spent most of the next day luxuriating in my crinkled, wrinkled sex sheets. A girl tends to do that when she hasn't had any for over 365 days. Oh my God, I could hardly believe that I had actually done *it, and* that it was good enough to keep me smiling until Nicole came over with my lottery tickets from the party.

While we searched casually for my million-dollar ticket, she commented on my good spirits. "That party was a good idea. It's been a long time since I've seen you so relaxed." I debated for a second about whether to let her in on my secret. I would bet my yet to be found million dollars that she wouldn't approve of my sexcapade. Nicole tended to be a little conservative, but I couldn't keep my mouth shut.

"It wasn't *just* the party, girl." The coin that she was using to "scratch off" was still in the air when she looked at me suspiciously.

"What are you talking about, Fee?" I scrunched

my face up like it was going to hurt me to say what I was about to say.

"Well, when I got in the cab I realized that I had left the heel of my sandal in the club, so I had the driver take me back to get it, and that guy was still there."

"What guy?"

"The guy who caught me when I was falling off the table." Nicole's eyes lit up and she clapped her hands together gleefully.

"Oh my God! He was gorgeous! Did you make a date with him? You gave him your number? What?" She was genuinely excited for me. Nicole had been saying for months that I needed to get out there. But of course, I knew what happened the night before was not exactly what she meant; in fact, it wasn't at all what she meant. She meant that I should get out and *meet* men, get to *know* a man.

Nicole *refused* to accept the fact that the last thing I wanted to do was get to know a man. I knew everything that I needed to know about men: They were all the same. I almost regretted bringing it up, but who else was I going to tell?

"We had sex!" I blurted out, then held my hands protectively over my head as if she was going to hit me.

"What!" It was not a question, it was an expression of horror. I lifted my hands and looked at her as contritely as I could.

"Well . . . I needed a ride." *In more ways than one . . . ba da boom!* "We had a great conversation on the way over, and well . . . it just *happened.*" *Liar, liar pants on fire.* I couldn't tell her the whole truth; it had been a carefully orchestrated, though somewhat drunken, plot. Nicole was not only conservative, she was judgmental. She closed her eyes for a minute and I could tell that she was trying to get it together and suppress her natural instinct to judge.

"You needed a ride? But I put you in a cab." She waited for me to explain.

"Well, I had to go back to get the heel from my sandal." Doubt was all over her face.

"Why didn't you have the cab wait for you?" She should have been a lawyer.

"I didn't think of that."

"Yeah, right. Well, I hope you used a condom, Fee."

"*Of course we did.*"

"I'm not going to say anything about how dangerous it is to let a *stranger* into your home." *Let the judging commence.* But I was not going to let her ruin my good spirits. I smiled at her and clasped my hands together as if I was about to pray.

"Please, Nicole, I've thought about all that. Can you just let me savor my good memory?" She made a "do what ever you want to do" sound with her mouth and went back to her pile of scratch-off tickets.

We worked together silently scratching the coating from the tickets. We put the winners in one pile and the losing tickets in another. When we finished, the winnings totaled $2,100—enough money to cover the cost of the party *and* buy that Fendi bag I had been debating over. I could feel Nicole getting more excited as the dollar amount grew.

"Girl, you lucked out." She smiled at me.

"I told you last night was my lucky night." I stood up and did a little "free money" dance. She laughed out loud then, and I knew she was ready to forgive me for being less than an angel.

"You are *so* crazy. Since you risked your life for a little piece, I hope the brother had the 'mandatories.'" Her sly comment about the "mandatories" let me know that she was ready for details. After a series of unsatisfying sexual relationships in college, Nicole and I had each made list of the "mandatory" physical attributes a man had to have in order to be a good lover.

I said she was conservative and judgmental, I didn't say she was a nun. And by the way, the series of unsatisfying sexual relationships I just referred to was no more than one or two . . . three max. It wasn't as if we were skipping around campus screwing just anybody. Well, come to think of it, Nicole was, but I wasn't. I looked down at her from where I was standing.

"First of all, the piece in question was everything *but little,* and the only other thing I'm going to say about it is that *rough tongue* has now been added to my 'mandatory' list. Nicole fell back in her chair laughing.

"You just now adding that to your list?" She sat back up in her chair and we high-fived each other. We cleaned up the small mess we made, and I offered her a drink. As we walked in the kitchen I asked about her day.

"Why aren't you at work? You playing hooky, too?"

"I went in this morning, but I had to get out. Sometimes that place just drains me." I could have kicked myself for asking. Nicole was the director of a drug rehab center, one of the only ones in the city that provided shelter for the children of the women seeking treatment.

Recently, whenever she talked about her work, she theorized that most of the women didn't want to stop drinking or doing drugs, how they didn't know how to care for their children properly, and that the mandatory parenting classes were a waste of time. That was discouraging talk coming from a person whose job was to *believe in* and help the women she had become so disdainful of.

I knew what the *real* problem was, and so did she. It wasn't her job or the women. Nicole had been trying to get pregnant for close to two years, and seeing so many children in need of stable parents every day was a constant reminder of what was missing in her life. She sat at the small bistro table in the kitchen while I took lemonade from the refrigerator.

"You know the girl Renata I told you about a while back? Well, anyway, we just found out this morning that *she's* pregnant. She hasn't been clean eight weeks. I swear, instead of going to the fertility specialist, I need to be going to the crack house. Shit, I'd probably get pregnant with triplets." I laughed at her comment and gave her the glass of lemonade.

"You need a break."

"I need a *baby*." She said the words with conviction. I took the glass right back and held her hands in mine.

"You're going to get your baby, Nicole. The doctor said there's nothing wrong with you and there's nothing wrong with Anderson. I know it's hard, but you just need to let go. How many times have you given me the same advice?" She half laughed half snorted and picked up her glass again.

"I know, but I *would* be the only damn black woman in the Carolinas with fertility issues." We both laughed over drinks. "Well, at least I'm a respectable married woman and not a 'ho.'" She looked at me pointedly and we both laughed again. Fortunately or unfortunately, I had never been a "ho" and we both knew it.

"*One* one-night stand does not a ho make."

"You're not planning on seeing him again?"

"No! I pretended I was asleep when he got up to leave. He left three numbers on a piece of paper on my nightstand. *The girl still got it!*"

"Well, if it was good for you, and he wants you to call him . . . why don't you?"

"*Because* . . . I'm not *trying* to see him again. It was just a one-night thing to dust off the sexual cobwebs." I sounded a little defensive even to my own ears, but I continued, "He could be Jack the Ripper's play brother for all I know, and even if I was interested, he looked a little *old* to be cleaning tables at a club."

Nicole gave me a disapproving look. "I think it's a big mistake to judge a man by what type of work he does. I mean, in the long run, what does it matter what his job is? Just as long as he's *working.*" I looked down at her and raised my eyebrow in disbelief.

"I guess it wouldn't matter if you're *Mrs. Dr.* Anderson Jordan." Her expression went from disapproving to contrite in about two seconds.

"True, true." She laughed and went to put her glass in the sink. "I stand corrected."

But I wasn't ready to let the conversation drop. "But in *this* situation, you're right. I don't care if the man is a CEO or GDO. Men are just too much work, and in the end, they just screw you over."

"*Hello!*" Nicole waved her arms frantically in the air as if I couldn't see her. "Happily married woman still in the room."

"I know you're happy, Nicole. I pray that you never have to go through what I went through, and that you and Anderson have eight babies and live together happily ever after. I'm just saying that *I'm* not interested in trying to make it down that road again. I've had *enough.* Just the thought of giving a man control over my emotions again . . ." I had to shake the image away; just thinking about it made me sick to my stomach.

"Have you ever heard the expression 'a man's place is in the bedroom and in line at the ATM'?" I asked her.

"No, I haven't." She laughed and shook her head from side to side.

"I know you haven't, 'cause I just made it up. But you get what I'm saying. From now on, Nicole, any personal contact that I have with men will be strictly sexual . . ." I thought for a minute then added, "Maybe an occasional dinner or a movie thrown in for appearance's sake, but that's it." She scrunched her face up doubtfully.

"Yeah, right. And how long do you think that will last?" I looked her straight in the eye with no hint of a smile.

"For the rest of my life." I was *very* serious. We stayed in the kitchen talking a while longer, about her job—which in all actuality, she loved—about our families, and about all the other little things people who have known each other for most of their lives talk about.

As she was getting up to leave, she looked at me and asked, "What is a *GDO*?" I had to think for a minute before I remembered what she was talking about. A short laugh escaped me before I could answer.

"*A goddamn opportunist!*"

CHAPTER 5

Oone of the senior partners at my firm was married to a woman whose niece was married to a man who had a problem taking things that didn't belong to him. Apparently, he was dismissed from his last job, because—after several warnings—he continued to steal the lunches of his coworkers from the employee refrigerator. He had no choice but to admit that he was, in fact, stealing the lunches, because on several occasions he had been caught eating the lunches in question. *Ridiculous, I know.*

Because he was related, through marriage, to a partner in a major law firm, he decided that he should sue the company for unlawful termination. "Yes," my boss suggested that I argue, "he *did* steal the lunches, but thievery is the main symptom of the disorder from which he suffers. Because of his disability, he should have been given the opportunity to take advantage of the company's mental health benefit before he was unduly terminated." I knew the argument was a stretch, but until I reached a certain status at the firm, many such cases would come my way. I was hoping to settle the case quickly, all the man wanted was enough money to pay for treatment.

Opposing counsel suggested we meet for lunch to discuss a settlement offer; he would bring his client, the owner of the small company, and I would bring my client, the sack lunch bandit. I am getting to why all of this is relevant.

We arranged to meet at a restaurant that was convenient for all parties. I saw my client, a superslim man with black hair and Howdy Doody freckles, walking toward the front entrance of the restaurant just as I was pulling into a parking space. I couldn't help but feel sorry for the man. I mean, what could he have been thinking?

I checked my makeup before stepping out of my vehicle. "Leonard!" I called out to him. He looked around confused until he saw me. I hurried across the concrete to where he waited. The pained expression on his face caused me to smile reassuringly at him.

He didn't say hello; instead, he started a somewhat nervous ramble. "Do you think we can settle this thing today? We *really* need to settle this thing today. My wife is threatening to divorce me. This is the third job I've lost because of my problem since we married eighteen months ago." I placed my hand on his shoulder for a minute to calm him.

"First, Leonard, I'm advising you not to mention that this is not the first time you've had problems in this . . . uumh, particular area, and whether or not we settle today depends on how much they're offering." My words seemed to relax him.

"Well, then, it'll be settled today." He sounded confident. We made it to the front of the restaurant and I stopped and faced him directly.

"Leonard," I warned gently, "your case is weak; we'll be lucky if they offer you a few thousand dollars to cover the cost of treatment." His smile held steady.

"If they offer a couple of hundred dollars, that's fine with me. I just need them to acknowledge that I have a problem and that they shouldn't have fired me. If they don't, my wife and family will continue to think that I'm *just crazy*. I need people to know that I have a legitimate disorder." He said it with the passion of a crazy man. I considered telling him the truth for just a minute— that he was crazy—but professionalism won out.

"Leonard, two hundred dollars won't cover this *lunch*. I assumed you wanted money for *treatment*." His look told me that I had assumed wrong.

"It's not about the money, I have lots of money. My family is very wealthy. Your firm will be compensated fairly. It's the *principle* of the matter," he stressed to me as if I were the crazy one. I thought my boss was doing a favor for a relative; knowing my boss as I did, it made more sense that the relative would be rich. Leonard's eyes appeared to glaze over as he continued to talk about his "obsession with sack lunches" and how it had started in first grade.

The only way I could hold my tongue was to close my lips firmly over it. For every minute that I had to spend with him, *listening to nonsense*, I decided that I would figure out a way to charge

him for *two*. You know what they say about a fool
and his money . . . you know, they're soon parted.
In this case, the same would apply to a more-
cash-than-he-knew-what-to-do-with, sandwich-
stealing, crazy man and his money.

I smiled tightly at my client and motioned for
him to walk through the door of the restaurant
before me. Suddenly, I didn't feel comfortable
walking in front of him.

All thoughts of our conversation left me when
I stepped into the restaurant. I was immediately
impressed by the décor. Actually, I was blown away.
Vibrant color coated the walls. The furniture was
a clever mixture of modern and contemporary.
I felt right at home. Six original-looking Charles
Eames wood lounge chairs lined the wall of the
waiting area. Molded plywood screens separated
several tables toward the back of the restaurant,
giving the patrons the illusion of privacy. Exotic-
looking light fixtures hung from the ceiling.

I recognized the furniture because I had always been interested in design and architecture.
I had a few pieces at home—some Heywood-
Wakefield, a Barcelona chair, and a Knoll table.
Eventually, my plan was to furnish my home almost completely with the beautifully clean pieces
of the 1950s and 1960s.

The hostess allowed me to gawk for a minute
longer before she had someone show us to our
table. If the food was half as good as the décor, I
decided that I would only charge the lunatic at
my side for services rendered.

Chester Ford stood up to greet us as we approached the table; Marshall Dodge (not his real

name), his client and my client's former employer, continued to sit, and, in fact, refused to make eye contact with us when we sat down.

"Mr. Dodge," I said, *except I used his real name*, forcing him to look up at me. "Sorry that we meet under such unfortunate circumstances, but hopefully we can settle this matter quickly." I gave him my warmest smile and picked up one of the menus on the table.

I really didn't give a damn whether we settled the matter. It was, after all, a very frivolous lawsuit. All I was interested in at that point was whether the menu was as exciting as the décor. And as my grandfather used to say, I was "red to eat."

But before I could even peruse the appetizer menu, my lunatic client burst out, "I want five hundred dollars and a letter addressed to my wife telling her that I have a legitimate disorder."

Mr. Dodge shot back without deferring to counsel. "I'll give you two hundred fifty," he stated flatly. "And what significance would a letter from me have for your wife? I'm not a doctor." I looked over my menu pointedly at Chester as the two men hashed out the terms of the settlement on their own.

Leonard's voice took on a pleading quality. "I know you're not a doctor, but my wife really likes you. Tell you what . . . Give me one hundred fifty dollars and the letter and we'll be done."

Mr. Dodge looked at his lawyer, who nodded his head almost imperceptibly.

"You've got yourself a deal."

My client smiled as if he had won the lottery and reached over to shake the hands of both men. "Great! Lunch is on me."

I couldn't help but smile at him; there went his $150 plus, but so long as he was satisfied my job was done.

A very attractive woman approached the table and informed us that she would be our waitress; actually, she said, "I'll be your server this afternoon." It was *that* type of restaurant.

I ordered apricot tea and told her that I thought the restaurant was very beautiful. The men ordered drinks also. When our "server" brought our drinks back to the table, I mentioned the décor again.

"Do you have any idea who did the interior design?" She smiled politely and told me that she had only worked at the restaurant for a short while but offered to ask the owner after she took our orders. I ordered a grilled turkey and cranberry sandwich and sweet potato fries and handed her my menu.

The men at the table talked man talk after they ordered while I continued to look around the restaurant. I crossed my fingers mentally; if the food was any good, I was going to be a regular.

"Hello . . ." The voice coming from behind my chair startled me for two reasons: first, because I was deep into my own thoughts, and therefore was not aware that someone had approached the table, and second, because the voice was embarrassingly familiar. "Marla, your server, told me that someone at this table asked about the designer." He was standing behind my chair, and I couldn't see his face. I *could* see his face if I turned around, but I didn't want to turn around. I wanted him to go away.

My crazy client spoke up when I didn't. He looked at me pointedly. "Didn't I hear you ask something about a designer?" I gave Leonard a tight smile and turned slightly in my seat so that I could see the person standing behind me.

"That would be me." I was very proud of the way I kept my composure when I actually saw his face. It was him! The man that I'd slept with— excuse me, *had sex with*—the night of my divorce party. Leave it to me to run into a one-night stand at a business lunch. I could tell that he remembered me by the slight smirk on his face. The other men sitting at the table probably thought that he was smiling politely, but I knew he was smirking.

He had on a denim chef's coat with CHEF NICK stitched across the left side. He didn't look like a chef. Most of the chefs that I had seen on TV had quite a bit more around the midsection. And though his midsection was covered by the coat, I vaguely recalled that he looked *aww-ight* with his shirt off.

"I asked the *waitress* if she knew the name of the designer." He smirked a little more.

"That would be me. Nick Nathaniel, owner and executive chef of Nathaniel's."

So! I hoped he didn't think I was impressed I was, but I hoped he didn't think so.

"Oh . . ." I said disinterestedly. "Well, thanks." I turned back to the others and prayed that he knew a brush-off when he got one. Apparently, he didn't. I could hear the smirk in his voice when he spoke again.

"But I do have the name of an excellent designer if you need one. She's helped me with several other projects. If you'd like to leave your number with me, I'll pass it on." The men at the table gave each other knowing glances. I spoke to him without looking, rather rudely I hoped.

"No, thank you." He had the audacity to put his hand on the back of my chair, never mind that his hands had touched things way more personal than my chair.

"You look very familiar." He kept his hand on my chair but moved slightly to the right so that he was in my peripheral vision. I had no choice but to smile at him, but I kept it tight.

"I get that a lot," I said, then turned pointedly back to the men at the table, who at that point appeared to be very interested in the limited exchange between myself and the owner of the establishment. But he (the owner of the establishment) wouldn't let it go.

"No, really . . . There's something very familiar about you." I turned around to give him a death stare, but he looked *really* puzzled. Either he was a chef, a restaurateur, and a very accomplished actor, *or*, it suddenly occurred to me, he just might not remember me. I was torn between being relieved and being insulted. Insulted ground relief into a fine powder. I mean, I know I hadn't put my *best* moves on him that night, but damn!

"Excuse me." I made my voice as sweet as my mama's candied yams. "We're right in the middle of a business lunch. We're actually very pressed for time." He smiled at all of us and apologized for interrupting. When he was out of hearing range,

Chester, the other lawyer at the table, was the first to speak.

"Looks like you have an admirer, Fiona." I was going to ignore the comment, but the sandwich swiper chimed in.

"I'm sure Fiona has plenty of admirers. She's a very beautiful woman." He had the audacity to raise a suggestive eyebrow at me. The look that I gave him caused him to lower his eyebrows immediately and the other men to chuckle.

As we were continuing to work out the details of the "settlement," the server approached our table with a very expensive-looking platter and placed it and small serving plates in the center of the table. I looked with admiration at the four enormous crab cakes that were placed artfully in a creamy seafood sauce. "We didn't order these," I told her. She smiled.

"Compliments of the chef." As soon as she said that, my companions gave each other knowing looks and grabbed their plates. The server handed me a slip of orange paper that had been folded in half and stapled. "Also from the chef," she said before leaving again. I should have put the paper in my purse, but I'm very curious by nature.

As the men made sex noises over the shellfish, I unfolded the paper as discreetly as possible.

I know women like to play hard to get, but I've already had you, remember?

The words were printed in a very neat masculine handwriting on the center of the paper. I was not amused. When I looked up, my companions were staring at me expectantly.

"Care to share?" asked the sandwich swiper.

"Just the name of the designer he mentioned." I shrugged my shoulders casually, folded the paper, and placed it in the pocket on the side of my purse. The men had demolished three of the crab cakes and my client was going for the fourth. "Would you like some bread with that?" I asked sarcastically. He stopped just as he was about to scoop the last one up with his fork. His expression was sheepish.

"I'm sorry, Fiona. Would you like one?"

"No, thank you." My appetite was gone and all I really wanted was to get out of the place. I decided that I would stay until our entrées arrived; then I would plead a headache and leave. As the plan was forming in my head, our server approached our table again, not with our food, but with another beautiful tray. This time she placed a frosty glass in front of each one of us.

"The chef again," she said. And again, she handed me an orange slip of paper. I took a sip of the concoction, a frothy peach lemonade, before unfolding the note.

> *Meet me in the open area next to the kitchen.*
> *I need to talk to you.*
> *It's very important. If you're not there in less than five minutes I'm coming to get you.*

When I read the word "important," I started to feel a little panicky. The only *important thing* one-night standers could have to say to one another, in my opinion, had to do with disease.

And I was absolutely sure that our sex had been as safe as sex can be, or at least as safe as it can be when two people are actually having *sexual intercourse*. Nothing too freaky-deaky, no exchange of bodily fluids, but still, I was nervous as I made my excuses and my way toward the kitchen area.

He was leaning casually against the wall as I approached. Members of his staff were bustling in and out of the kitchen. He looked good, better than I remembered. I hadn't allowed myself to get a good look at him when he stood at our table.

I gave him a hard look before speaking. "Do you make it a habit to harass your patrons when they're trying to conduct business in your establishment?" He ignored my question. "What's so important?" He smiled at me.

"I just wanted to let you know that's it's not too late to call. Sure, my feelings are a little hurt, but it's nothing that dinner and good conversation won't mend."

I decided to be direct. "I didn't call because I had *no intention* of calling. I didn't even *look* at your number before I threw it in the trash." *Direct . . . brutally honest . . . What's the difference?* He laughed and moved aside to avoid being run over by a young man carrying a silver pitcher.

"Too much for you, huh?"

I looked him up and down. He was wearing jeans under his denim coat. The material touched his muscular thighs. A wide white smile revealed a long dimple in his left cheek, and his skin was tan over brown. He looked fresh.

"Absolutely not," I said disdainfully. I snorted

just a little bit to further illustrate how way off the mark he was. "Now, if you'll excuse me, I have a meeting to get back to." As I turned to leave he stopped me by grabbing my wrist. His warm hand on my skin caused my heart to beat a little faster.

"Take your hands off me!"

"Off was not where you wanted my hands the last time I saw you," he whispered. Did I mention that his teeth were not just white, they were gleaming? When I didn't smile at his comment, he tried another approach. "Look, I'm just saying I was disappointed when you didn't call, and when I saw you walk into the restaurant I knew that I had to speak to you before you left. I was thinking of a reason to approach your table when Marla said that some people were asking about a designer." I raised a perfectly arched eyebrow at him.

"Is that your way of saying that you *do* normally harass patrons in your restaurant?" He laughed again. Obviously he wasn't affected by my "directness," so I tried another tactic. I showed him *my* pearly whites, and then lowered my head slightly and shook it as if I was embarrassed.

"I'm sorry if I've been rude. It's just that I was a little bit tipsy that night." I held my thumb and index finger up to make the "itty-bitty" sign and caught my bottom lip between my teeth, still revealing the top row of my pearly whites. "I decided to just put that night behind me. Now, if you don't mind, I'd like to finish my meeting so that I can put it behind me also." The expression on his face became friendlier.

"You can tell me all about it over dinner."

"Tell you about what?"

"Your meeting, why you want to put the night we had together behind you. You can tell me your shoe size, your favorite color . . . *anything*. Just have dinner with me."

He was very charming I had to admit, but I continued to hold firm.

"I can't have dinner with you."

"Why not? I know you're not married, and judging from your behavior when last we met, I don't think you have a boyfriend . . . or at least I hope you don't."

I sighed big. I didn't have a real reason that I couldn't have dinner with him, and my inner voice wouldn't stop chanting, *dinner with the possibility of a screw . . . Go ahead what's wrong with you?* I let out another exaggerated sigh.

"If I say that I'll have dinner with you, will you let me take care of my business without any more interruptions?" I nodded my head back toward the general direction of my table. The light of victory was in his eyes.

"If you promise to have dinner with me and *mean* it, there will be no more interruptions from me, I promise. Scout's honor." He held up a suspicious-looking scout sign. I suspected that he had never been a Boy Scout.

"Okay," I said and turned to walk away, but again, he grabbed my arm.

"I'm going to need your name and a working phone number." I held up one empty hand as I shook free of him.

"I'm going to need a pen."

He stepped into the kitchen and after a few seconds reappeared with pen and paper. He handed it to me. I jotted down the requested information and gave it back.

"Fiona is a beautiful name. I guess at some point you'll feel comfortable enough to tell me the rest of it." I had been away from my client for at least eight minutes; I had to get back. The expression on my face told him so. "I know you have to go. I'll call you later this evening to make arrangements. I nodded my head in agreement and turned to walk away. This time he didn't stop me.

CHAPTER 6

Three days later, I was standing in front of the mirror in my closet trying to decide what to wear. *What exactly does one wear for dinner and dick?* Something tight to make him salivate over the lush curves of my body, or something loose to give him easy access to the lush curves of my body? Salivate good, easy access not as good. I decided on tight.

I dressed quickly before I had a change of heart. When I was done, I stood back to look at myself. The superslim super-low-cut jeans and the lightweight black turtleneck leotard was perfect. The outfit said *maybe you gonna get some . . . maybe you ain't.* I pulled my thick hair up into a bun, put on my second largest pair of silver earrings, my reddest lipstick, and my blackest mascara. I took my favorite leather jacket from the closet—it wasn't cold outside, the jacket just went well with my leather boots—and I was ready to go.

Nick had suggested we meet at his restaurant.

I figured that we would have dinner there; then he would invite me back to his place to watch a movie or "something." I blasted my favorite CD during the twenty-five-minute drive to the restaurant. I was not nervous at all about the "date." I was discovering that the best thing about being interested in a man for medicinal purposes only was that I didn't spend any time stressing over the kind of impression that I would make on him.

The parking lot was empty, except for the catering van that Nick had taken me home in on the night of my party and a *long* black Mercedes. I checked the time and the date on my watch. Right date, and it was five minutes before we had arranged to meet. Either the restaurant was closed or business was very slow.

I parked my truck about five spaces down from the van and got out warily. *What is going on?* I wondered to myself as I pulled on the front door of the place. It was locked. I pulled the door again to make sure and it wouldn't budge. I looked at the discreet sign right above the handle. The place was not open for dinner on Thursday; it was Thursday, and it was dinnertime. The man had played a cruel trick on me. Cruel because though I was not *nervous,* I had been thinking almost obsessively about the "or something" that was sure to have come after dinner.

My boot made a hard noise on the concrete as I turned to walk away. I muttered and cursed him and myself on the way back to my truck. How dare I travel even five minutes from my house at the suggestion of a stupid-ass man? A man who couldn't be counted on to show up for what he had to know was probably a sure thing. I felt like a damn fool! Wasting my gas and my time . . .

"Fiona!" I turned toward the deep voice shouting my name. It was Nick. He had on a black button-down shirt and black tailored slacks. The top three buttons were open, revealing soft-looking hair. I remembered how that soft-looking hair had tickled my nose during our first encounter and I took a deep breath to calm myself. I had a slight frown on my face as I approached him.

"What's going on?" I demanded. "The door is locked. The parking lot is empty. I thought we were having dinner." He held up his hands defensively, but his smile was warm.

"Whoa . . . whoa. We *are* having dinner. The place is closed, but luckily I have the key." He put his hand on my back and pushed me gently in the direction of the restaurant. "I have a glass of wine waiting for you inside." I moved toward the door reluctantly. He was where he said he would be and he wasn't late, but I was still perturbed.

We walked into the dimly lit room, and as he helped me remove my jacket, I started looking around for a place to sit. He must have noticed because he gestured with a large hand.

"I'm just finishing up dinner; let's go into the kitchen. We'll eat in my private dining room."

His private dining room . . . Give me a break.

"Is there something wrong?" he asked.

"No, why?"

"I ask because you just *snorted,* and the expression on your face says that this is the last place you want to be. I hope you're not apprehensive about being here alone with me. I promise not to try anything that *you* haven't tried before." He was teasing me. What made him think he had the right to tease me? I snorted in a more ladylike manner, but I didn't speak. "Let's get you that wine right now." I followed him through the kitchen doors.

The kitchen was spotless. Stainless steel was everywhere. Well-worn pots hung from the ceiling. Two industrial-sized refrigerators flanked the left wall. There was not an inch of wasted space. A pot simmered on one of the burners. I had never been in a restaurant kitchen and I had to admit that I was impressed.

"Nice," I said quietly as he handed me the promised glass of wine. I sipped from the glass. The wine was light and crisp, and whatever he had simmering smelled delicious.

"I hope you like fish." He was stirring the simmering pot. I walked to the stove and peered in. *"That's fish?"*

He smiled indulgently and held out a sample for me on the wooden spoon that he was using to stir. "No, it's a special seafood sauce for the fish that I'm about to take from the oven."

"A *special* seafood sauce?" I asked skeptically. My skepticism turned to appreciation as he slipped the wooden tip of the spoon between my lips. The sauce *was* special. The buttery concoction practically melted in my mouth. "Ummm," I moaned, "that's heaven." He turned off the fire.

"Yes, it is. I call it sauce Fiona." He looked at me smiling, trying to gauge my reaction. I curled my lip at the suggestive light in his eye. I knew better than to be flattered.

"Yeah, and I bet last week it was called sauce *Betty* or *Karen*."

"Close, but it wasn't last week, and it was sauce *Stephanie*." He was ushering me into a private room as he spoke. I couldn't help but laugh at his little joke, or maybe it wasn't a joke . . . either way, it was funny.

The room was decorated beautifully. I had to give it to him, the man had excellent taste. A table in the far left corner of the room was set with crystal and silver. The champagne-colored tablecloth caressed the hardwood floors. Two small chairs were positioned in front of a flat-screen television. Books and vibrant art glass were positioned strategically around the room. I noticed that all of the custom furniture was on wheels. In essence, it was a beautifully appointed studio apartment; the only thing missing was the bed. He picked up a remote control and suddenly I was surrounded by soft jazz.

"Sit down anywhere and enjoy your wine. I'll be back in a few minutes with dinner." He didn't wait to see which seat I chose. I walked to the dining table for a closer look. The tablecloth was made of very fine linen. The place setting was beautiful. Three plates of various sizes were stacked on a silver charger. I lifted the first plate and turned it over. The name of a very well-known, very expensive designer was scrawled across the rim. *Well, looks like he went all out to impress you, girl,* I thought to myself.

"I see you have a thing for plates." Nick's voice startled me. The very expensive plate that

I was holding slipped from my hands and onto the other plates. I knew without looking that something was broken.

"Shit!" I said when I looked down and saw that two of the plates were completely broken and the bottom plate was cracked.

I heard him wince slightly before he spoke. "Don't worry about it. What's a couple of hundred dollars when you're trying to get to know someone?"

I was immediately defensive. "I'll pay for the plates."

"Okay." He put the bottle of wine that he was holding on the table and starting picking up the broken china. *Okay? Does he really expect me to pay for his overpriced plates? I don't think so!*

"You startled me. You said you'd be gone a few minutes," I said, and waited for him to respond.

He gave me a strange look, then spoke slowly, "I *did* say that, and *then* I decided to bring the wine in here. I hope that was okay?" His implication, of course, was that he didn't need my permission to come into his private area in *his* restaurant. The mild sarcasm was not lost on me. It was going to be a long evening. If that sauce hadn't been so good I would have made some excuse to leave. Instead, I smiled sweetly at him and offered to help clean up the dishes.

"I have it," he said. "Why don't you sit on the *sofa* until I come back with dinner." I deliberately sat down on one of the chairs, not the sofa.

While I waited for my dinner, I continued to look at the beautiful objects positioned around the room. I also took that time to revise my game plan. The plan was simple: I would eat and leave.

A man who expected a woman to pay for a broken dish didn't deserve any sexing from me. He was too concerned with material things, I decided.

Whoever heard of a man spending money on designer dinnerware, never mind that he was a restaurateur? Which brought up another possibility: He probably got the dishes at a substantial discount and was probably going to try and charge me full price.

I had almost convinced myself that the sauce wasn't worth the aggravation when he wheeled in a steel cart loaded with food. I forgot my train of thought and jumped up . . . I mean, I stood up *leisurely* to examine what was on the cart. He replaced the broken dishes and put equal portions of the redfish with sauce Fiona, slender asparagus, and scalloped potatoes on each plate. He said "dinner is served" with such warmth and hospitality that I went back to my original game plan—*dinner and dick.*

I know I was running hot and cold, but I hadn't been on a date in almost ten years. I was trying to listen to my intuition . . . another thing that I hadn't done in almost ten years.

We sat down for dinner, and I was a little put off when he said a short grace. I normally didn't say grace before eating. Not that I wasn't grateful, but I figured that since God is omniscient, he already knew the extent of my gratitude; plus, personally, I feel that fornication and faith are an odd mix. *One at a time, please, one at a time.*

My "amen" was a bit awkward, but he didn't seem to notice. I closed my eyes after taking the first bite of the fish; it did almost as much for me as a good kiss. The potatoes were equally delicious; the taste of sharp cheese, rosemary, and garlic exploded in my mouth. I was about to sample the asparagus when he decided to make dinner conversation.

"So tell me about yourself, Fiona." I wanted to say, *Look, man, I'm here for two things and neither one of them begin with the letter* c. Though if I substituted "cuisine and coitus" for "dinner and dick," then both of the things I was there for would begin with *c*. As I thought about it, I realized that there were a couple of other *c* words that I wouldn't be averse to exploring before the night was over . . .

"I'm a twenty-nine-year-old divorced lawyer with no kids. My favorite color is green, and if I were an animal, I'd be a bird." His smile stayed in place.

"Well, I'm a thirty-eight-year-old divorced chef with *two* kids. My favorite color is orange, and if I were an animal, I'd be a chameleon." I wanted to know why he would choose to be a lizard, but I wasn't going to ask and he didn't volunteer. "Now that we know *all* about each other . . ." I heard the mild sarcasm in his voice again. "What do you think of the food?" I was happy to talk about something less personal.

"The food is excellent. I didn't really get the chance to sample it the other day." I looked at him accusingly, but he looked unconcerned. "To be honest with you, I would normally choose meat over fish—"

He interrupted, "So is it safe to say that you're a big meat-eater?" His eyes sparked with mischief and a chuckle escaped me, despite my best effort to keep the cool, sophisticated, I-am-not-here-to-be-charmed-by-you expression on my face.

"Ha ha." I shook my head and rolled my eyes at his juvenile double-entendre, but I couldn't get my lips to stop smiling. "As I was *saying*, fish has never been my first choice . . . but I think I may need to start reconsidering. Where did you get your training?" He took a sip from his glass. "I've always loved to cook. My parents had a café all the while I was growing up. You may have heard of it: Pat's Prime?" He waited for me to respond.

"Yes . . . I've eaten there! When I was growing up my mother used to bring home biscuits from Pat's . . . she would slather them with apple butter . . . and *oh my God* . . . they would melt in your mouth." *Okay*, I warned myself, *too much enthusiasm for the biscuits.* He must have thought so, too, because his eyebrow was slightly raised. "I *really* like biscuits," I explained with much less animation.

Nick took another sip of wine before continuing, "Both of my parents were exceptional cooks. My mom made the biscuits from a hundred-year-old recipe. She called them "round doughs" instead of biscuits. He smiled in remembrance. We talked some more about the café. He told me that they served the biscuits for Sunday brunch at Nathaniel's. The conversation was going well, and I was starting to relax.

"It closed a few years back, didn't it?"

"Well, actually, when both of my parents were killed in a car accident, I sold the café and used the money to start this restaurant. That was five and a half years ago."

The more information he gave me, the more I wanted to know. I wasn't trying to get to know him. I am just a naturally curious individual.

"What did you do before you opened the restaurant?" I asked.

"I was an architect. Correction, I am *still* an architect. It just so happens that my last project was the redesign of this building. Cooking is my first love, but art and architecture . . . modern design"—he shrugged his shoulders—"they run a close second."

I started to tingle just a little bit. *I love art and architecture and modern design. Not a good sign!*

"How did you make the leap from architect to chef?"

He smiled and chuckled. "I can tell you're a lawyer. If I didn't know better, I'd think you were cross-examining me. But to answer your question, counselor, it wasn't such a big leap. The food that I serve is practical, reasonably priced, and beautifully presented. I feel that I've created an atmosphere that's serene *and* exciting. I did the same thing when I designed and supervised the construction of housing with New Urban Ideas." He dropped the name of a well-known design firm in the Durham area.

The firm had received a number of awards and positive press for doing just what he said—making beautiful and affordable housing. I had read a number of articles about the firm, because like I mentioned before, I'm interested in architecture and shit. As he continued to speak, I started to feel "frowny" inside. We had too many common interests . . . again, *not a good thing*.

"An *architect* is a designer and creator of buildings and spaces. A *chef* is a designer or creator of foods. I'm doing the same work, it's just a different medium." The expression on his face was intense. The look was almost sexual . . . but that could have been me.

"I can tell you like what you do." I smiled politely at him and picked up my fork. His laugh sounded a little embarrassed.

"I do like my work . . . I always have. I've been extremely blessed in that arena." *Another reminder of "church" things.* "But I don't like to be a conversation hog. Tell me about your work."

I shrugged my shoulders as if to say, "What's there to tell." "I'm a lawyer. I go to court. I try cases. Sometimes I lose, but most of the time I win."

He wiped the corners of his mouth on his napkin and placed it back on his lap. "I see you like holding your cards close to your vest. Do you like being a lawyer?"

I did. I *loved* being a lawyer! I was *born* to be a lawyer! I was voted most likely to be a lawyer by my senior class in high school (a category that I, editor of the yearbook, suggested). I graduated at the top of my class from Duke Law!

"I like it." I said it with about one-sixteenth the enthusiasm that I had expressed over his dead mama's biscuits. But he didn't give up.

"What do you like about it?"

I tried to make my voice sound as shallow as the words. "I like the money. I like wearing nice clothes to court. I like the fact that people are normally impressed when I say, *I'm a lawyer.*" His booming laughter caught me off guard.

"That's funny . . . that's really funny. I know

that's not what attracts you to law. I watched you after you went back to your table that day, and you were really into whatever it was that you were discussing. But I like that . . . I like a woman with a sense of humor." He looked at me for a long time . . . well, for about three seconds, but it *seemed* like a long time. I was feeling "frownier and frownier." I went back to eating my food, hoping that he would get the message and just *shut up*! He was ruining the evening for me with his intelligent conversation and good humor . . . not to mention that damn dimple. He appeared to be more relaxed, and he leaned in closer to me.

"How long have you been divorced?" Talk about an out-of-the-blue question.

"My divorce was final ten to twelve days before my divorce party." He looked sympathetic.

"Speaking of your party. I have to say I found it very unusual. I've never heard of someone *celebrating* a divorce. I would think that it would be difficult to talk about it so soon afterward. And there you were . . . giving a party."

I smiled tightly at him before asking, "Then why are you talking about it?"

He scrunched up his face in apology. "I'm sorry. If it's a sensitive subject right now . . . believe me, I understand."

"No . . . It's not a sensitive subject," I said somewhat sensitively. "It's a short subject. He screwed me over, I left him, and a year later the divorce was final. End of subject."

"Infidelity is a hard pill to swallow. Did you know the woman?"

"I never met her, but she was his secretary or

something like that." I didn't feel comfortable discussing the situation with him, so I tried to sound curt and cut into my asparagus. Apparently, I didn't sound curt enough, because he just wouldn't change the subject.

"Are they still together?"

He is one thickheaded . . .

"I don't know." This time my voice held little expression. "But last I heard she still worked for him. I anticipate she'll be in his employ *forever*. Where else is he going to find someone who'll work for a few thousand dollars a year and all the dick she can suck?" Nick choked on the piece of fish that he had just put into his mouth. I looked at him wide-eyed and innocent as his violent cough caused his eyes to water. *Calm down! I would have offered him some assistance if he had been in any real danger.* When his coughing subsided, I asked, "Are you okay?"

"Yeah, thanks for your concern." I heard sarcasm in his voice, but I ignored it and took a sip from my wineglass. He sipped from his own glass before speaking again. "I think you may have had your party too soon. I heard a lot of bitterness in that last comment."

"Oh . . . so you're a chef, an architect, *and* a psychologist?" He laughed, but I could tell by the way his eyes narrowed that he didn't like my comment.

"No, I'm not a psychologist, but I've had enough experience with matters of the heart to know bitterness when I hear it."

"I'm not bitter; however, I don't like the fact that I was betrayed by someone close to me, and I don't feel I have to pretend otherwise." I had not discussed my divorce and my feelings surrounding it at length with anyone other than my closest friends. The fact that he was lingering on the topic was making me very uncomfortable. I didn't like it.

"But what about *you*, Nick? How long have *you* been divorced? What happened with *your* marriage?"

He sat back in his seat and sighed an *"it's a long story"* sigh. "We met in college and married right after. Over the years we grew apart. I was working hard trying to build a career, she had her own career plans . . . she's an administrator at Duke. We didn't have any common interests other than our kids. Our communication wasn't what it should have been." He shook his head as if it had been a sad sad situation. "Eventually, we both decided that a divorce was probably the best thing." He was about to say something else, but I could no longer hold back my laugher. I laughed until tears formed in the corner of my eyes. "What's so funny?" He had the nerve to sound offended. I had to take several calming breaths before I could speak.

"So, in other words, you were screwing around?"

His eyes narrowed even more. "When people grow apart—"

I *had* to stop him. "Look, Nick, I don't know if you realize it or not, but you just offered me almost every excuse in the book. You married too young . . . she didn't understand you . . . you grew apart . . . you didn't have anything in common . . . The only excuses you haven't offered are that the two of you were *sexually incompatible* and that old standby, *she let herself go.* All *I* need to know is, were you or were you not fucking someone other than your wife prior to your divorce *and* was adultery a precipitating factor in the aforementioned divorce." I stared him straight in the eye, challenging him to tell me what I already knew.

"I did slip up," he admitted reluctantly, then said, "I'm not offering any excuses," before offering me another excuse, "but my affair was a culmination of everything that was going wrong in my marriage." I looked at him doubtfully.

"I don't know your ex-wife, but I'd be willing to bet that when she speaks about *her* divorce, she tells people that you were screwing around before she gets to the part where the two of you were growing apart." He put his napkin on the table in a "I've had enough of this" gesture.

"You're right . . . You don't know my ex-wife, and you don't know me. I tried to put together a nice evening for you . . . thought possibly that you could be an interesting person, but I should have known better than to try and date a woman who would take a man home and fuck him when he didn't even know her name."

I inhaled sharply and dramatically, then covered my mouth briefly with one hand as if I were shocked and offended . . . *I was neither.*

"You know, my feelings would be really hurt right now if I gave a flying fuck about the opinion of a man who would fuck a woman without knowing her name." I lowered my voice about three octaves. "But as it is, it's all gravy."

"*It's all gravy?* Did they teach you that in law school?" he asked sarcastically.

"Yeah, as a matter of fact, they did." My answer was equally sarcastic. "I got a million of 'em."

He pushed his chair back and stood up. "This is ridiculous. Obviously this was not a good idea . . . you seem to have a problem with men and—" I interrupted him. "Correction, not all men . . . just adulterous men." I couldn't resist. I saw the light of amusement shine briefly in his eye.

"So you're a lawyer *and* a smart-ass?"

"Like I said, I got a million of 'em. And by the way," I said as I stood up, "I'm not paying for those bourgeois designer plates."

"I didn't *ask* you to pay for the plates, you *volunteered.*"

"Well, I'm *un*volunteering," I said smartly. "Now, if you'll wrap my food up for me, I'll get out of your way." His mouth parted slightly in disbelief.

"You expect me to send food home with you?"

"You invited me here for dinner, didn't you? I barely had three bites of my food before you starting grilling me. It's not my fault if you didn't like what I had to say."

"You have some real issues. You keep them wrapped under a beautiful package, but they're there. I think it's best if you just leave." I looked down at my plate and, for a moment, considered grabbing it and making a run for the door. Instead, I shrugged my shoulders, lifted my purse from the small table in the center of the room, and walked out without saying another word.

I was glad to see keys dangling in the door. I was able to let myself out without asking for his assistance. Once I was outside, I glanced at my watch. The entire date had lasted a grand total of forty-one minutes. Things had definitely not gone as I had anticipated. No dinner and no dick . . . damn, and I was hungry for both.

Maybe I should have been a little less caustic. I couldn't recall ever behaving like that before . . . certainly not with a virtual stranger. But he didn't help matters in my opinion, insisting that I pay for those plates, asking personal questions about my divorce, lying about his, making fun of my profession, and suggesting that I need psychological help. *Men!*

CHAPTER 7

I was just about to step into my truck when I heard keys rattling in the distance and Nick calling out my name. "Fiona." I ignored him and pulled the door open. "Fiona, I know you hear me. You forgot your jacket." Damn! I put my purse in the seat and turned and stretched my hand out for the jacket. He gave it to me and I turned back around.

"Before you leave, I need to apologize." *Damn right you need to apologize.* I turned around again. My expression said *"I'm listening."* Under normal circumstances, I would have just gotten into my truck, but the circumstances were far from normal. "I made some comments that were uncalled for." He paused and looked expectantly at me. I guess he expected me to apologize, too, but I didn't feel like it.

"Your reference to the night I met you *was* uncalled for. I wasn't trying to win your respect or approval, and I won't be judged by you or anyone."

"I'm glad you said that. I feel the same way," he said pointedly. "I think we both said some things we shouldn't have said." I ignored his inference that I had something to do with the fast demise of what was supposed to be a pleasant evening. I hadn't said anything that I was sorry for.

"If you were offended by my actions that night, maybe you shouldn't have interrupted me when you saw me with my client."

"I didn't say I was offended by your actions. To the contrary, I was very pleased at how the night ended for both of us. Honestly, I was disappointed when you didn't call me. I don't know about you, but I feel like the level of passion we experienced that night was special. Hell, the little argument that we just had stimulated me." Another good thing about not caring about a man's opinion or approval was that I was free to be totally honest . . . well, almost.

"I prefer to do my arguing in the courtroom. And as far as that night goes . . . the sex was *good*, but I can't exactly say I experienced new heights." He laughed. "Then why did you agree to see me again?"

"Because it was *good*, and I'm not adverse to experiencing it again. And if I'm going to eat, I may as well eat good food." I could tell he didn't believe me. "*I'm serious, Nick.* I just finalized a divorce. Nothing personal, but the only *new* thing I'm trying to experience right now is doing what *I* want to do for the first time in my adult life. I'm not looking for a boyfriend; I'm not looking for a soul mate." Even the word "soul mate" sent a shudder through my body. "And I'm not looking for a psychologist."

"What *are* you looking for?"

I shrugged my shoulders. "Nothing." It sounded a little crazy even to me, but it was the truth. I was looking for nothing, and I wanted him to know that if "something" came along I didn't want it and wouldn't use it. He nodded his head slowly as if he understood.

"Would a reheated dinner fall under the umbrella of nothing?"

I nodded my head. "But let's make sure the conversation doesn't get so personal this time."

"So you're agreeing to a truce." I nodded my head again and closed the door to the truck. "Wait a minute," he said as I started to move away from the truck. "I think we should kiss and make up before we go back in. You know, make the truce official." The smile on my face was wide.

"I have no objection to that."

He moved in close enough to pin my body against the door. I sighed when he opened his lips over mine. The kiss was long and sweet. He was the first to try and break contact, but I wrapped my arms around his neck to make him stay.

"One more," I demanded against his mouth. And he kissed me again before leading me back into the restaurant.

We finished our dinner and two bottles of wine without further incident. Our conversation was

limited to the weather and what team would probably go all the way in the upcoming baseball
season. He told me that he had the private dining
room built so that his kids would have a place to
sit, eat, do their homework, and watch TV on
nights when he had them but couldn't leave the
restaurant.

I even allowed him to talk about the rising price
of real estate in Durham, and I didn't protest
when he told me a funny story about his son.
We both told silly jokes, and before I knew it, I
was having a very nice time.

When dinner was done, he excused himself
and returned shortly with a different bottle of
wine. He sat on the small sofa and patted the
space next to him to indicate that I should join
him. "Grab your glass," he said as I stood up. I
did and took the seat next to him. He took my
glass and filled it to the rim with a sparkling
amber wine.

"Are you trying to get me drunk?"

"Do I have to?" he asked casually as he filled
his own glass.

"No, you don't." I allowed my eyes to linger
on his face for a moment before I drank deeply
from the glass and placed it on the coffee table.
It was time to get down to business. "Where's
the nearest bathroom?" He pointed to a closed
door on the other side of the room.

The bathroom was miniscule—toilet, sink, and
the smallest shower I had ever seen. There was
very little room to turn around, but it was nice.
And everything, from the rust-colored toilet with
the elongated seat to the hammered copper
sink, looked very expensive.

After using the facility, I peeked into a mirrored cabinet and looked for some toothpaste. I squeezed some of it on my index finger and rubbed it briskly over my teeth and tongue. My eyes were a little cloudy from the wine, but I was thinking clearly.

Since he didn't have a bed, I had spent some time during dinner trying to determine the most comfortable place for us to carry out the second part of my plan. I didn't want to invite him back to my place, and I didn't want to go to his. The sofa was too small, and though my ex and I had waxed a couple of floors in our younger days, the thought didn't appeal to me anymore. The simplest thing, I decided, would be to straddle him on one of the dining chairs.

The tight jeans had not been the right choice, after all. It was going to be very difficult to look sexy while removing my boots, the jeans, and the turtleneck with nothing to support me but furniture on wheels. I should have worn the dress.

Standing in front of the mirror, I remembered that I was the new, improved, advanced formula Fiona. I took off all of my clothes except for the panties that were much too pretty to be left on a cold bathroom floor. I took a deep breath before stepping back into the room.

Nick stopped fiddling with the CD player and stared at me. Actually, he looked me up and down, and I believe I heard him mutter "damn" softly under his breath. "I hope you don't mind," I said, openly acknowledging my nudity. "I splashed water on my clothes . . . they're wet . . . so I left them in the bathroom to dry." I lied with a big smile on my face.

"What about your panties?" He questioned as he forgot about the music and walked toward me. "Are they wet, too?" *This man and his innuendos . . . I swear!*

"No," I said primly.

He pulled me close, and the soft silk of his shirt felt good against my skin. He kneaded my shoulders and back with large, warm hands; then he kissed me. Nick slid his tongue on top of mine and caressed the roof of my mouth. When he was done pulling and sucking on my lips and tongue I was breathless, my knees were weak, *and* my panties were wet.

He slid his hands from my shoulders to my wrists, then caught my hands in his. Nick held me at arm's length as he looked again at my body. He moved his head slowly from side to side. "You are so fucking beautiful . . . so sexy." I remembered that he had said something similar the first night we were together. I *felt* beautiful and sexy.

Though I hate to give him any credit, I couldn't deny that sex with my ex-hole had been . . . decent. He had known what buttons to push to get me "there." But with him I had never felt so erotic, so much like anything goes. Nick said what I was thinking.

"I don't know what it is, but there's something about you." His words and the way he said them sent me into overdrive. I jerked him back to me and put my tongue in his mouth. I kissed him hard and long as he moved his hands down my back to knead the firm flesh that my thong panties didn't cover.

He slid two very important fingers along the side of the silk and elastic, and when he found what he was looking for, my knees buckled slightly. "Let's sit down," I half moaned half muttered against his lips. He stood back from me again, but this time unbuckled his belt and unzipped his pants and let them fall to the floor. The shirt came off next, and then we were equals. Him standing in front of me in white cotton briefs, with the object of my desire bulging toward me; me standing in front of him in a black silk thong, wet and waiting.

It didn't take him long to pull me back into his arms. His fingers found their position again, and this time he moved them in and out of me like he knew everything there was to know about me. "Let's sit down," I begged urgently. I was really about to fall . . . I could feel it! But we didn't sit down. He backed me against the wall and moved his fingers before he whispered against my ear.

"You know what I want to do? I want to lift you up and fuck you right here against this wall. You're so wet and I'm so hard . . ." He moved his hands to the side of my hips and started pulling my panties down. When they fell, I stepped out of them quickly.

"Do you want this dick?" He had moved my hand to the front of his briefs . . . the material was hot.

"Yeah, I want it." I looked him in the eye as I spoke. "You know I do."

"Then take it out," he instructed. I moved my hand upward and pulled back the elastic band of his briefs. I used my hands and fingers as deftly as he had used his, squeezing a little, stroking a little, making him moan *a lot* before I finally did as I was told and pulled it out.

I pulled the shorts away from his hips and let them fall to the floor. Then we were naked. The full length of his body touched mine. He kissed the side of my neck and teased my ear with his tongue. At the same time, he buried his hands between my legs and squeezed and stroked and searched until I stopped moaning and started panting.

"I want to feel you just like this. I want to slip inside you right now." He moved my hands from where they were resting on his shoulders, and I felt how wet and slick his fingers were. Nick forced my hand down and I closed it around him. "I want to be inside you just like this," he said. I knew what he meant, and I panicked for a second.

"No!"

He stroked the sides of my shoulders and moaned away my protest. "Calm down, Fiona. I said I *wanted* to, I know I can't." He kissed me some more and I forgot about everything. "I'll be right back." He nibbled on and whispered against my lips. My eyes shut on their own accord when he stepped away from me. When I opened them, he was pulling the covers back on a plush-looking queen-size bed that had appeared from nowhere. I was amazed.

"Where did that bed come from?"

"It's a Murphy bed. It's built into the wall. I just pulled it down," he explained. I was familiar with the Murphy bed; I was just surprised to see that the little room was so well thought out. I thought fleetingly that there were probably many more women who had been surprised by that bed, but at that point, it really didn't matter. "Come here," he said when the bed was ready.

"What?" I asked as I walked toward him. He was sprawled across the bed. Muscles ran the length of his body, and his rich skin looked decadent against the creamy linens.

"Come over here so I can taste you." *Now how could I say no to that?* When I offered no objection, he instructed me further. He tapped his two important fingers against his lips. "Come and sit right here." *Again . . . how could I say no?*

I took my seat and placed my hands on the wall in front of me. Nick dug his hands into my ass and went to work. And damn if he didn't do it righteously (I know that's me mixing a religious reference with fornication, but what the hell!). He used his tongue to stretch and move me, and I slid around on his lips to maximize my pleasure and his.

"Oh! Oh! Oh!" Was all I could say. I found myself moving more insistently and pressing myself deeper onto his tongue as I came closer to the final "oh." And just as I was about to get "there," he broke our seal and moved from beneath me. My knees trembled against the sheets as disappointment caused me to open my eyes. I wanted to hit him, accuse him of being a tease, but he was in front of me before I could get my thoughts together.

"Why did you stop?" My voice was a whimper. He caressed my breast with his mouth before speaking.

"Because I know you want this dick, and I want

to feel you tighten around me when you come."
He jerked my legs down and I was in position.
He had put on a condom when I wasn't looking,
so he was free to push himself inside me in one
smooth motion. I lifted my legs instinctively and
closed them around his back. Nick moved in
and out of me slowly, but I didn't want it like
that and I told him so.

"Fuck me hard." I barely opened my mouth
to speak, but he heard. He moved in and out and
around with so much energy that I started crying his name. "Oh, Nick, Nick . . . What are you
doing to me?" Sweat from his forehead fell onto
mine. I wanted him to go on forever, but I couldn't
contain the feeling that had been building in me
since the early part of the evening. I had to let
go and let the sweetest, strongest orgasm sweep
through my body.

"I feel you . . . I feel you." I heard him say
over and over again before he pressed his lips to
mine and demanded a kiss. "Fiona, oh baby,
your pussy is *sooo* good . . . I'm about to come." I
ground my hips up into his in a way I knew
would push him in deeper. "Oh shit . . ." was the
last thing he whispered before I felt him shudder and fall onto my chest.

I enjoyed the heavy weight of his body for a
moment before he rolled over onto his back.
He placed one long arm across his forehead,
and the only sound in the room was the sound
of us trying to regain our composure.

"That was incredible," he said when he was
able. I didn't say anything because I hadn't re-
gained my composure. I decided that speech

was not necessary. I closed my eyes and drifted off to sleep . . . totally satisfied.

I don't know how long I was out, but when my eyes fluttered open, Nick was standing near the bed with a stark white towel tied around his waist and was holding a platter. I brushed the hair out of my face and allowed my eyes to adjust to the dim lighting before sitting up. Cheesecake, strawberries, chocolate sauce, and utensils were arranged neatly on the platter that he was holding. At that moment, I didn't have any problems with the man.

"Dessert," I sighed and sat up straighter. He let his towel drop and joined me under the covers. "You sure know how to spoil a woman," I teased. *It's funny how good sex can put you in a good mood.* "Fight with me, feed me, fuck me, and then feed me again." I winked at him playfully to let him know that I approved. I dipped my finger into chocolate sauce, but before I could bring it to my mouth, he captured it between his lips and stole the chocolate.

"That's four *f*'s," he said before feeding me some of the cheesecake. "Lucky for you, I'm into odd numbers."

CHAPTER 8

So Nick and I fell into a little "nothin' nothin'." We started hanging out together on a regular basis—a movie here, dinner there, a couple of concerts, and the most satisfying sex I have ever been an active participant in.

He was a pretty decent guy as far as guys went. I found out that he was really into his children, and that he eventually wanted to open more restaurants, and that his favorite word was "alleviate." He was always finding a way to throw it into the conversation like, "This is the best aspirin for alleviating a severe headache," or "The city needs to do something to alleviate this traffic problem." Don't ask me how, but one night he used the word eleven times in a three-hour period. I thought it was kind of cute.

Now, I know what you're thinking. You're thinking, *Watch out, Fiona, that's how they reel you in; they spend a few dollars on you, compliment you, and try to mesmerize you horizontally—or in Nick's case, horizontally, vertically, and asymmetrically—and before you know it, you start believing what he says, you start wondering what he's doing when he's not with you . . . you start staying over at his house, and then BOOM, your heart is broken.*

I appreciate the concern, but that's not going to happen to me. First of all, my heart has been permanently hardened to that "he's different from all the others" bullshit. And second, I have safeguards in place. Now you're wondering, *well, why does she have safeguards if her heart is permanently hardened?*

I will gladly address the question. Though I'm not stupid, I am a flesh and blood woman with feelings and emotions. I have *safeguards* to make sure that those things don't have the opportunity to rear their naive little heads. Now you're thinking, *Poor Fiona, she is so disillusioned.* Yes, I am, and gratefully so. I would rather be disillusioned than *deluded* . . . again. You can use that if you like.

I call my safeguard "Fiona's Foolproof Formula for Fabulously Frivolous Fucking." The rules are as follows:

1. Always practice scrupulously safe sex . . . except, well . . . uumh . . . I mean . . . you know . . . let's just move on to the next one.
2. Never see each other more than twice a week.
3. Stay away from the important friends and family members of your *"associate,"* and keep him away from yours.

4. Do not sleep over . . . Do not allow him to sleep over. Get your ass up and go home! Always wake up in your bed—alone.
5. *Last and most important,* Never forget that he's a man.

For the past several weeks, I had adhered to the rules and everything was going great! Not just with Nick, but also with my job, my family, my hair, everything! I was doing things that I have always wanted to do. Speaking of doing things that I've always wanted to do, Nick had invited me to see Alvin Ailey American Dance Theater. Whenever they've come to Durham, I've made plans to see them, but something always came up, but this time I was definitely going.

The best thing about going out with Nick— well, one of the best things—was that he was so well-connected in the city. When something comes to town, not only is he *invited,* he's invited to the preperformance cocktails, to the postshow gala, the prescreening brunch; in other words, he had VIP status. And because he was my "fucker," I enjoyed the same status whenever he invited me to one of these events.

His invitation to see the dance theater included the reception before the show. Some of the key dancers were supposed to be present for mixing and mingling. Otherwise, I would never have agreed to go, because he was bringing his kids along.

What? His daughter wants to be a dancer, and he has his kids pretty often during the week. It wasn't not like he was bringing them along so they could meet me, and I was just going for the entertainment and free food.

The day of the performance, I worked double-time so that I could go home and relax before it was time for me to get dressed. A picture of what I was going to wear had popped into my head as soon as Nick mentioned going to see the dance troupe.

I had gone on a big-ticket shopping spree about six months into my separation. I bought my BMW, my town house (my ex-hole still thinks I'm leasing), a Chanel bag, a Judith Leiber purse, a Rolex (not platinum), and a new wardrobe complete with shoes and perfume. I put most of the items on credit cards, so he ended up being responsible for about half of the stuff I bought. Now, don't try that unless you have a really good divorce attorney.

Anyway, I had a couture dress that was perfect for the evening's festivities. . . . Well, it wasn't actually couture, but it *was* designer. The wide skirt was perfectly pleated white shimmering silk, and it fell just above my ankles. The tuxedo-style top was made of the same silk and draped softly over the elastic band in the skirt. The skirt was very sheer, but not so sheer that I would consider it indecent. The designer had strategically placed pockets made of a more opaque silk over the breast area. I had felt like a chocolate Marilyn Monroe when I tried it on in the store. I had twirled until the skirt fanned out around my waist, and it fell quietly back into place as soon as I stopped. I knew then that I had to have it.

When I got home from my office, I took the dress out of the closet and laid it across my bed. For a moment, I had second thoughts about wearing it. I had forgotten that the dress was not just sheer, not just very sheer, but very very sheer. The memory of how I had looked and felt in the dressing room kept me from putting it back in the closet. It was perfectly appropriate . . . at least *I* thought so, and what else mattered?

My sister called and Nick rang the doorbell at the same time. I normally avoided speaking directly to my sister. When she called I let the answering machine get it, and I only called her when I was sure she wouldn't be at home. We did most of our communicating via our mother. But when I picked up the phone to check the caller ID, I inadvertently pressed the Talk button.

"Fiona?" She sounded exasperated.

"Yes, Ramona?"

"Why haven't you returned my calls?"

Nick rang the doorbell again just as I was about to answer her. "I'm coming," I shouted in the general direction of the front door, at the same time I grabbed the evening bag that I was carrying that night at the bar.

"Fiona!"

"Yes, Ramona, what is it?" She sounded more exasperated than she had ten seconds before.

"I can hear that you're busy, so I won't keep you. I've started participating in a Bible study group for divorced women. And I wanted to invite you to one of our meetings."

"Thanks, Ramona," I said without giving the invitation any thought, "but I'm busy that night."

"I didn't tell you what night we meet." Damn, I had spoken too soon!

"I mean I'm busy in *general*. Look, Ramona, I have to go. I'll call you later." I hung up the phone just as she was about to say something. I turned off the ringer before I put the phone back on its base. Ramona couldn't stand to be cut off, and more than likely she would be calling back in the next five seconds or so.

Purse in hand, I went to open the door for Nick. I greeted him with a semiapologetic smile. "Sorry it took so long, but my sister called when you rang." He looked good in his lightweight navy slacks and sports jacket. His shirt was ice blue and contrasted nicely with the jacket.

"No problem," he said slowly. "Are you ready to go?" The way he said it and the way he looked down at my clothes caused my eyes to tighten *just a little bit.*

"Yes, I am." My voice was firm. I waited for him to turn and walk back to the car, but he remained in the doorway.

"I *did* tell you that my kids are going with us, didn't I? They're waiting for us in the car." He sounded confused as he nodded his head back in the direction of his car. I nodded my head yes but didn't say anything. He looked me up and down again, this time more pointedly. "Do you think it's a good idea to wear something so revealing?" I looked down at the silk pockets covering my nipples. *Revealing?* I couldn't see anything.

"I'm fully covered, Nick. I admit the dress is sheer, but it's not see-through. The most provocative thing your children or anybody else will see is the *silhouette* of my legs." I could tell he thought he was being diplomatic when he spoke again.

"Fiona, you're not wearing a bra, and your top is unbuttoned almost to your naval." I left him standing in the door and walked to the mirror behind the bar as if to carefully revisit my clothing choice. I turned back to him while still standing in front of the mirror.

"You're right, Nick. I'm sorry. What was I thinking?" I buttoned one button and smoothed the pleats over my hips before turning back to face him. "*Now* I'm ready," I said; my tone was mild, but the expression on my face was not. Nick shook his head from side to side before he spoke.

"Let's go, then. I'll be in the car."

CHAPTER 9

The night was a disaster! I should have slammed the door on him when I saw the look of fatherly disapproval on his face. By the way, that's another thing that men start doing after a while, they start trying to control what you wear. They start off by innocently pulling the sides of your classic polka dot Diane Von Furstenberg wrap dress together and saying, It's a pretty dress, but next time you wear it, you may want to pin it together." Then they ask you, Why do you always have to wear a thong, when they were the one who bought you your first one. My ex-hole used to do that shit, and I was not about to let Nick start. If you're smart, you'll watch out for that.

Anyway, like I said, the night was a disaster. Nick introduced me to his kids before he pulled away from the curb. Nathan, his 8-year-old son, and Noelle, his 13-year-old daughter, did not appear to be particularly pleased to meet me. I tried to be pleasant to them, even though I was more than a little perturbed with their father.

"Hi," I said, and extended my hand into the backseat. The daughter showed me the coolest smile that I had ever seen come from a 13-year-old, and I'm not talking cool as in "groovy"; I mean cold, and oddly . . . what is the word I'm looking for . . . *scary* comes to mind. She did brush the tips of her long, thin fingers against my palm; the boy, however, ignored my outstretched hand and headed straight for the jugular.

His exact words were, "Gross! I can see your nipples." Of all of the adjectives he could have chosen, why "gross"? Why not "superior" or "damn!" . . . a simple "wow" would have been more palatable.

Before I go on, let's consider the following questions: first, what 8-year-old uses the word "nipple"; second, why didn't his daddy correct him, instead of snickering like *he* was 8 years old; and last, this is not a question, I just want it on record that the little boy was lying . . . he could not see my nipples. MY BREASTS WERE COMPLETELY COVERED!

Anyway, Miss Noelle chastised her brother when her father said nothing. "Nathan, that was rude! She's an adult, if she wants her nipples to show, that's her business." *Thanks a lot.*

I turned around in my seat and gave their father the evil eye. My mother believed fiercely in the power of the evil eye and had warned my sister and I on numerous occasions to use it with caution, but I spit caution down the side of his neck and waited expectantly for his leather seat to trap and squeeze him like a boa constrictor. I only gave him the evil eye for a few seconds before regaining my composure. I didn't really believe that a dirty look from me could cause him to have an accident, but you never know . . . and I *was* sitting next to him . . . and, oh . . . of course, I didn't want anything to happen to his kids in the backseat.

I took a calming breath and decided to try once more with the children. I turned toward the backseat again. I would not address their inappropriate comments about my lady parts. "You guys look great," I said, and honestly they did. They were beautiful children.

Noelle had on a simple two-piece black and white linen pantsuit. The tiny studs in her ears were probably real diamonds. I couldn't see her shoes, but I was sure they were nice. Her hair was pulled high atop her head in a loose pony tail, and she had on lipgloss and a hint of mascara.

Nathan was dressed in dark slacks and a light blue dress shirt. There were two jackets on a hook in the backseat. I recognized the one his father had on earlier, and I assumed the smaller one was his. He looked like how I would imagine his father looked at his age.

"How was school today?" I was proud that my voice sounded like the adult voices that I remembered from *Sesame Street*.

"It's summer," the two beautiful but irritating children said in unison. They said it as if they had been waiting all of their lives to correct me. I knew it was summer, for all they knew I could have meant *summer* school. I could feel their father's amusement.

No further attempts at conversation were made, so we rode to the Performing Arts Center in silence, except for the ringing and buzzing that was coming from some handheld video game that the boy was playing.

Nick opened the door for me with a smile on his face. His smile was infectious, but I held my jaw in place as I stepped out of the car. His children got out without his assistance and ran ahead to the elevator at the far end of the parking garage. Nick warned them to slow down. He slithered next to me and spread his hand wide in the small of my back.

"If I tell you that you look beautiful, will you show *me* your nipples?" He could barely get the words out of his mouth before he started laughing. *I didn't see what was so damn funny.* I shook his hand from my back and walked up to join his kids. "Fiona, wait up! I'm sorry." His continued laughter told me that he didn't mean it.

When we stepped out of the elevator, I blinked several times in response to the brightly lit reception area. Chandeliers dotted the ceiling, and lush velvet seating was discreetly placed around the room. It was beautiful and I loved a beautiful room. After I had taken in the décor, I took a closer look at the other people in the room.

The room was full of men, women, and children, and none of them were dressed like me. Apparently, Nick had invited me to some sort of family night. The women were dressed in slacks or skirts with coordinating tops, flat shoes, and designer handbags. In my opinion, they looked like zombies. They were clinging to their men and casting motherly glances to the small clusters of children throughout the room.

Nathan and Noelle both asked permission before going to join some of the other children. "What exactly have you brought me to, Nick?" He smiled and waved at people he knew as he answered quietly.

"I told you, it's a fund-raiser for my kids' school." My head started throbbing then. Maybe he had told me, but I made it a point to only listen to half of the stuff he said. I certainly wouldn't have worn my dress if I had known that Nick was taking me to a damn PTO meeting. I needed a drink. Daddy dearest must have read my mind.

"Do you want something to drink, Fiona?'

"Yes, a cosmopolitan." He started walking toward the bar and I hurried up beside him. I didn't want to be left standing without cover. Nick looked down at me and there was a softness in his eyes.

"You *do* look beautiful, Fiona Lisa. Pretty as a picture." I allowed myself to smile back at him this time and even chuckled a little. I had revealed to him only days before that my mother had named me after the famous painting—the *Fiona* Lisa.

We sat down and had our drinks. Some of the excitement that I had felt earlier returned. So what if I was getting disapproving glances from the left and from the right. *I don't know these people . . . would never see them again . . . wouldn't recognize them if I did see them again, and I am minutes away from experiencing something that I had always wanted to experience.* Even his kids had disappeared; I was lulled into thinking the night could be salvaged. Nick and I finished our drinks and were just about to get up to find his young and our seats when a very tall and sophisticated-looking woman approached us. "There you are, Nick," she said with a slight sigh. "Noelle is going to sit with us, and Nathan wants to sit with his classmate Jordan. They wanted me to clear it with you." She waited for his response without acknowledging me. I assumed that she was his ex-wife.

She reminded me of a young Diahann Carroll. There were black embroidered flowers on her very expensive-looking lavender silk dress, and her hair and makeup were immaculate . . . as was her manicure and pedicure. Oh, in case I didn't mention it earlier, my hair and makeup were immaculate also.

I could tell at first glance that we were very different people with very different tastes. Though she *was* very beautiful, I thought she looked a little *unnatural.* I preferred a lighter hand with makeup, and I thought that a black and purple dress with black and purple sandals, earrings, *and* handbag was a little girlish. To be totally frank, she was the kind of woman who a person looks at and just naturally assumes that she is a bitch. *Not me, though! I* didn't make snap judgments about other women, especially not ex-wives.

Nick's face tightened. "That's fine, Yvonne, just have them meet me back here after the performance." Yvonne's face took on a fake half-frowning expression.

"They want to go back home with Graylon

and I. I can drop them off at your place first thing in the morning if you plan on being there." She looked pointedly at me for the first time. I smiled politely at her . . . she did not return my smile.

Nick introduced us. "Yvonne, this is Fiona, Fiona this is my ex-wife Yvonne." I held out my hand and Yvonne brushed her fingertips across my palm as her daughter had done earlier.

"Yes, the children told me that you brought along a friend." Her voice held a hint of amusement. I could just imagine what *the children* had told her. I didn't like her tone or her expression. Like I said, I don't make snap judgments about other women, but I am a lawyer, and when presented with evidence—however circumstantial— I can usually assess a situation accurately. I couldn't say beyond a reasonable doubt that she was a bitch, but she was definitely in the bitch realm.

Nick shook his head politely. "I don't know about that, Yvonne. I'll talk to the kids after the performance. I didn't expect to see you here tonight." *I hope he wasn't implying that he wouldn't have brought me if he had known that she would be attending.*

"I helped organize the event, Nick . . . of course I would be here." She sounded a little exasperated. "I'd like to speak to you in private if it's all right with your *friend.*" She was looking at me as if Nick had picked me up at the bus stop, but I smiled at the skinny *bitch* and nodded to her in a very ladylike manner.

"Excuse me, Fiona." Nick followed Yvonne to a corner a few feet away from where we had been standing. I tried to appear as though I was comfortable standing alone in the middle of the brightly lit room, but I was beginning to feel self-conscious. Nick and Yvonne were having an intense conversation. I tried not to eavesdrop, but when I heard the words "embarrassed" and "inappropriate" my ears perked up. As their parents continued their conversation, I saw Nathan and Noelle approaching with a smiling man.

"Where is my dad?" Noelle asked me. I pointed to her parents standing in the corner and she went to join them.

Nathan stood before me drinking something from a supersized cup, and the smiling man introduced himself. "Hello, I'm Graylon, Yvonne's fiancé."

"I'm Fiona, nice to meet you," I said with *no* enthusiasm. He was what my mother would call "decent looking"—clean-cut and very thin like his wife-to-be. We stood awkwardly watching Nathan sip his red concoction until the other three joined us.

"It's settled then," Yvonne said with satisfaction. "The kids are coming home with us tonight, Graylon." She looked down at Nathan. "Maybe before you go back to your dad's in the morning, Graylon can help you practice on your skateboard." Though her words caused Nick's face to tighten even more, from the corner of my eye I saw little Nathan jumping and squealing.

I was watching Nick's facial expression with great interest, *he was very unhappy about something*, so I didn't see exactly what happened. I felt a sudden splash of something icy cold on my bare toes, and the bottom part of my light as air dress felt heavy and wet. I saw the cup that Nathan had been holding roll across the floor, and everyone around me was still for about five seconds. I didn't need to look down to know what I would see, but I did anyway. Crushed red ice had landed on my toes and the part of Nathan's drink that was not on the floor was on my dress.

In his excitement, he had let the sweating plastic cup slip through his hand. My dress was ruined! "Nathan! Look what you've done." Nathan's eyes were wide and waiting, his mother's expression was slightly apologetic, Noelle looked as if she could give a damn, and Graylon kept smiling. I knew without having a mirror in front of me that I looked *pissed*.

"I'm sorry, Dad!" *Dad?* His dad didn't pay for my dress.

"It's all right, Nathan," Nick sighed. "But you need to learn to be more careful." *All right?* Again his daddy did not buy my dress.

I stepped out of the red puddle, and Yvonne took Nathan by the hand. "Nick, the show is about to start, Graylon and I will go and get the kids settled." She gave me another "I'm so sorry" look, and her fiancé waved to us. Noelle stood on her toes and gave her father a kiss on the cheek. They went on to enjoy the show that I had been waiting to see for almost twenty years. Nick watched their backs for a minute before turning back to me.

"I'm really sorry about this, Fiona, but you know how clumsy young boys can be. Let me get some club soda and some napkins for that stain."

"No, I *don't* know how clumsy young boys can be." I realize my response wasn't very gracious, but you'd understand if you knew how much I'd paid for my dress. "I *do* know this evening was a mistake, and that I want you to take me home right now."

"Fiona, it was an *accident*. I think you're over-reacting. Let's just go and find our seats." Of all the things he could have said . . . should have said . . .

"I'm not so sure it *was* an accident, Nick, and I don't give a damn if it was. You have insulted me. Your kids were rude to me, and you didn't do or say anything about it. I want to go home! Are you going to drive me, or should I call a cab?" My hand was on my hip, and my head was moving from side to side. I *also* didn't give a damn about the backward and sideways glances we were getting from the *"Parent Teacher Organization Moms and Dads."* Nick looked at me with narrowed eyes.

"I think you should call a cab." *Oww* . . . I *also* didn't expect him to say that. My hand went kind of limp on my hip, and I hesitated a moment before speaking.

"Fine," I said, then spun around like Michael Jackson. I was walking briskly toward the elevator when I realized two things: one, I didn't have my cell phone, and two, I only had twenty dollars cash in my small evening bag. Using a public phone would be no problem, but I was not about to call someone to rescue me, so my only choice was to moonwalk my Michael Jackson ass back to Nick and ask him for some cash.

Nick was about to get another drink. I fixed a polite and neutral expression on my face before tapping the shoulder of his sports jacket. He turned around to face me and lifted a questioning eyebrow.

"I need cab fare," I stated simply. The slow smile that spread across Nick's face was not there long before it turned into a full laugh. He reached for his wallet, still chuckling. He took out a hundred-dollar bill and held it out for me. When I reached for the money, he snatched it back.

"A little advice before you go, next time you try to make a dramatic exit, be sure you have everything you need." I reached up and snatched the money from him and turned my back on his amusement. He was no gentleman, I decided; if he had been, he would have at least *tried* to convince me to stay.

CHAPTER 10

I would not return his phone calls, I did not respond to his e-mails, and I refused to recognize the flowers that he sent to my office on two occasions. I'm talking about Nick, of course. For fourteen straight days after the dress/dance disaster I refused to have anything to do with him. I will now highlight some of the events that took place during those fourteen days.

Both my mom and my sister bugged the hell out of me during those fourteen days! Well, they didn't bug all the hell out of me, because according to some close personal friends, there's plenty of hell in me to spare.

The light was blinking on my answering machine when I got home that night. I was sure it was Nick offering some fifteen-cent apology. There was no message from Nick, but there were two *more* messages from my sister, one rather aggressive message from my dear mother, and one from Nicole thrown in the mix.

* * *

"Fee, this is Ramona, you didn't have to cut me off like that. I know that you're a busy career woman and all, but guess what . . . I have a career, too. I think it's important for us to support each other . . . especially at this time in our lives. If you would be so decent as to return my call, I would be grateful."

My sister taught science to ninth graders, and she showed as much enthusiasm for her job as she did for anything else in her life . . . *nada*. I laughed at the thought of Ramona and I supporting one another and deleted the message. My mother's message was next.

"Fiona Lisa Lawson Daniels or whatever it is you're calling yourself these days . . . pick up the phone!" Daniels was my maiden name. My mother knew full well that I had had my name legally changed back to Daniels during my divorce. *"I'm not your sister. I need to talk to you. You better call me back tonight!"* Next was a message from Nicole.

"Fee, what are you doing tomorrow? Anderson is going to a golf tournament, and I thought we could go for pedicures and lunch. They'll probably charge you double to work on your crusty feet . . . so I'll treat. Call me before nine tomorrow morning and let me know."

Just so you know, my feet hadn't been crusty since sophomore year in college, except during the first four months after me and my ex-hole separated, then they had been "get caught in the carpet" crusty. I made a mental note to call Nicole in the morning; a free pedicure is a free pedicure. I deleted the message and my sister's voice filled the room again.

"Fee, it's me again. I talked to Mama. She may be calling you about this, but really this is between us. I would like for us to spend some time together and get to know one another as women. It's really important to me, Fee. Do you think this is how our father would have us live out the rest of our lives?"

Our father? At that point, I didn't know what our father had to do with our relationship. Ramona was such a drama queen. She had the nerve to try and sound like she had been crying. I went into my bedroom and called my mom.

"What took you so long to call me back?" She practiced less than perfect phone etiquette.

I sighed and sat at the end of my bed. "I was out."

"Out with that man again? I hope you don't end up pregnant." *Pregnant? Where did that come from?* With my mother I had learned not to ask.

"I'm sure I won't end up pregnant, Ma. Is that why you called me?"

"No, it's not, *Miss Lady*. I called to talk about your sister. Have you talked to her lately?" I rolled my eyes toward the ceiling . . . Ramona had probably repeated our entire conversation to our mother.

"Briefly. I couldn't talk long, I was on my way out."

My mother sighed into the phone. "Well, you need to talk to her. She got herself involved in some sort of Christian cult."

"A *cult*? Come on, Mama." It was hard for me to picture my sister in a cult—She was just too damn stubborn and mean. We both had inherited from our mother an intense dislike of being told what to do.

My mother raised her voice slightly. "Of course they don't *call* it a cult. It's supposed to be some sort of church divorce recovery group. But she has to meet with those people on Sunday night, early Tuesday morning or Tuesday night, and on Friday at six o'clock they meet for donuts or some other shit, and they have to talk on the phone every day. You don't spend that much time with people unless they paying you, they screwing you, or they trying to get you into something you ain't got no business getting into." Now, that was the truth, but I still didn't believe my sister was in a cult, and the doubt was evident in my voice.

"Ramona is not in a cult, Mama—"

She cut me off before I could finish my sentence. "I *said* it's a cult, Fiona Lisa. Are you calling me a liar?" My mother had been asking me that question since I was four years old, and my response was always the same.

"No, ma'am." Her delicate snort said I didn't think so.

"Well, then, listen to what I'm saying. I don't really care what it is, but I know that Ramona shouldn't be spending all her time with a bunch of old, bitter women." I did listen. And I heard the real concern in her voice. "I don't want either one of my daughters to spend the rest of their lives punishing themselves and everybody else because their marriages didn't work out." I didn't really appreciate that comment. I knew it was aimed at me, and I wasn't trying to punish anyone. I was moving forward in my life. But I let it slide, because I knew she was upset, and I loved her.

"What do you want me to do? Ramona doesn't listen to anything I say."

"That's because you don't *say* anything. She told me that she invited you to one of her meetings. I want you to go and find out what's really going on." *And then what?* I asked myself.

"Okay, Ma, I'll call her back and tell her that I'll go with her."

My mother sighed with relief. "Good. Your daddy is starting his vacation on Monday, so we decided to drive to a bed and breakfast in Charlotte." My father had started as a carrier for the Postal system over two decades ago, and was now an administrator. He often said that my mother was the reason that he went to work everyday. My mother interpreted that to mean that he worked to be able to provide the things that she wanted in life. When he became eligible for retirement two years ago and continued to go to work every day, I interpreted it as something else.

"When will you be back?"

"We're leaving Sunday morning and we'll be back on Thursday night. I want you and your sister to come to dinner next Saturday." I was anxious to end the conversation and get ready for bed, so I didn't protest.

"Okay," I said.

"So I guess I can expect to hear everything that's going on with your sister that evening."

"I'll see what I can find out. I love you. Tell Daddy I love him, too. Have a safe trip."

"We will. I love you too, baby." I dropped the phone on the bed and went into the bathroom to get ready for bed. The mirror caught my attention. I discovered that if I stood very still directly under the light, I could make out a hint of nipple. I didn't care, though. Miss Noelle had been right about one thing: I *was* a grown woman, and if I wanted my nipples to show, it was my business. I slipped out of the dress and left it in a crumpled heap on the bathroom floor. After showering and brushing my teeth, I fell gratefully into a solitary night's sleep.

CHAPTER II

The day after my ill-fated date when I was ankle deep in sudsy water, I told Nicole that I wouldn't be going out with Nick anymore. "Oh no. What happened, Fee? He was so nice." I sat up straighter so that she could see my frown before relaxing back into my plush leather chair. My tone was casual.

"Who said he was nice? I rarely spoke about Nick." I could feel her eyes on me even though mine were closed.

"*Exactly.* And since I know your motto is, *If you can't say anything bad about a man, don't say anything at all,* I figured he must be nice." Damn, that was my motto!

"That's *not* my motto." I went on to tell her how his son had ruined my dress, and how I had to take a cab home, and how I could tell that Nick was very controlling, and that I didn't have time for any of that. She was confused by the time I ended my story.

"Wait a minute, could you repeat all or *some*

of what you just said, because none of it made any sense." I waved my hand at her dismissively just as the attendant took my feet out of the lukewarm water.

"Let's just forget it. I don't know why I brought it up. It's not important. I was spending too much time with him anyway. Next week I'll meet somebody new."

Nicole looked as if she wanted to say something but reconsidered. "If you say so. Speaking of somebody new . . . do you remember my cousin Samuel? He went to college in LA and stayed there?" I thought for a minute, then nodded my head. "Well, he's going to be in town next weekend. Can he call you?"

"For what?"

"Something to do with his job."

"No, I mean why should he call me?"

"*I don't know, Fee.* Maybe you can show him a night on the town or something. Do you have plans or can you meet him?"

I shrugged my shoulders. "Sure, have him call me."

She opened her mouth to say something else, but I put one finger to my lip to silence her. She wanted to talk. I wanted to relax and fully enjoy my foot massage. She spoke anyway. "You don't have to sound so enthusiastic," she said sarcastically.

I smiled at her. "Eventually, you'll have to believe me when I tell you that men no longer inspire enthusiasm in me."

* * *

I knew something was on Nicole's mind during lunch. She always sighed a lot when she wanted me to ask her if something was wrong. I knew I wouldn't be able to enjoy my Cobb salad and electric lemonade as long as she was sitting across the table from me breathing like she was about to have an asthma attack.

"Okay, I'll bite, what is it, Nicole?" She let out another long sigh before speaking.

"I'm just worried about you Fee."

This time it was me who sighed. "Why, Nicole? I'm fine."

She had on her social worker face. "You remember when we were about to graduate from elementary school and we went to the junior high for the battle of the bands?" she asked cautiously.

How could I forget? Almost twenty years later and the mention of that night still caused my stomach to churn a little.

Nicole and I had both played instruments in elementary school. I was clever with my clarinet, and she was fabulous with her flute. It was a longstanding tradition at Wetherbee Mills Elementary School for the sixth-grade band students to participate in the battle of the area junior high school bands. We didn't actually compete; we played one song, took our bow, and for the rest of the evening sat in the audience and listened to the competing bands.

Nicole's mom dropped us off at the junior high school. We were big girls, and at 11 years old, we didn't need our parents watching over us. Our hair had been greased, curled with foam rollers, and left down for the occasion.

After our performance, we sat down in the wooden auditorium seats. I was thinking that it was a good thing that we looked so good, because the room was filled with boys—*junior high school boys*.

Nicole and I and some other girls in our band were sitting and giggling quietly. We weren't paying very much attention to the bands because it was just *too* exciting to be hanging out with older kids.

A group of about four or five boys sat in the seats directly behind us, and all of us girls stopped our giggling and sat up straighter in our seats. My heart was pounding . . . I knew there was a reason that they sat behind us when they could have sat almost anywhere in the room.

Soon, the boys were making *pssst, pssst* sounds behind us. Of course, our excitement caused our giggling to start again. Then there were taps on the shoulders. One boy asked me my name, and I said *Fiona* like I was accustomed to boys asking me my name. I was vaguely aware that the other boys were trying to talk to my classmates, but with all the excitement it was hard to focus.

Nicole leaned sideways to whisper to me that the other girls wanted to go to the bathroom. I nodded my head yes. I knew us going to the bathroom was a ploy to get the boys to follow us out into the hall. I didn't know what we were going to do if they *did* follow us; all I knew was that I wanted to get a good look at the first boy who had asked for my name in *that* way.

I was at the end of the row so I stood up first. As soon as I stood up Nicole grabbed the hem of my brown flowered dress and pulled. "Fiona, that's okay," she said.

"Let's go," I said. Her wide eyes told me that she had chickened out, and I was instantly angry with her. I didn't look at the other girls who had also planned to go to the "bathroom" with us. She tugged so hard on my dress that I almost lost my footing.

"Just sit down, Fee!" she whispered harshly. I remember thinking that if I sat down I would look stupid, and that I wasn't going to let the fact that Nicole was chicken stop me from doing what I had stood up to do. I gave her a fierce look and yanked my dress out of her hand.

"I'm going to the bathroom," I told her. I stepped out into the aisle and started walking slowly toward the exit. I walked with a little extra sway in my still developing hips. I knew the boys would be looking at my butt, and I wanted them to know that I was a woman even though I was hanging out with a bunch of little girls.

I hadn't gone too far before I started hearing whispers behind me, then some giggles, and then cruel junior high school laughter. My feet slowed even more, because suddenly *I knew* why Nicole had tried to get me to sit back down. I considered running back to my seat, but the boys were still there. I had no choice but to walk the endless walk out of the auditorium. *You see that? Look at that girl? Ha ha! Hee hee* . . . followed me into the hallway.

When I finally reached the hallway, I twisted the elastic waist of my dress so that the back was in the front. My 11-year-old face crumbled when I looked down. Sitting in the auditorium, silently flirting, I had gotten my very first period. The pink and brown evidence was all over the flowers on my dress.

Nicole walked into the hallway, and I let the dress fall back in place. She had a "I'm so sad and embarrassed for you" expression on her face.

"I tried to tell you," she said quietly. Then she put her arms around my shoulders and we went to find a phone to call her mom. I never did get a good look at that boy.

I shook my head from side to side to clear the memory and focus on Nicole sitting across from me.

"Yes, Nicole, I'm sure when I'm old and senile that memory will be the last to go."

"You've always been like that, Fee," Nicole said delicately.

"Like what?" I asked, pretty sure that "like that" wasn't something positive.

"Hardheaded, stubborn, not really willing to listen to too much anybody else has to say. It just seems to me that these past few months you've taken it to a new level."

"You're right, I'm all of those things, but what does that have to do with the humiliating way that I started having my period?" I asked her.

"That entire situation could have been avoided. I was pulling on you trying to get you to sit down, but you *wouldn't*. You were determined to keep moving forward. I guess what I'm trying to say, Fee, is that when somebody who you *know* is a friend is tugging hard on your skirt trying to get your attention, take the time to sit down and listen."

"What an odd thing to say. Why did you say that, anyway?" She was determined not to let me enjoy my lunch. Nicole's expression was stern. She was often as hardheaded as she had just accused me of being.

"Because, Fiona, I'm tugging on your skirt now. Don't keep your dukes up so high. Every man that you meet is not going to be out to get you."

CHAPTER 12

I spoke to my sister and we arranged to meet at her house on Tuesday and drive to her meeting together. The official name of the group was "Sisters' Christian Recovery, Women of Divorce," in other words, *SCRWD*. They didn't call themselves that, and I think the irony of the acronym was lost on Ramona. The women called themselves "The Sisters." Ramona told me about her involvement with the group on the ride over.

The gym teacher from her school invited Ramona out to lunch with her and her cousin. During lunch she discovered that the cousin, Lacy, was recently divorced. According to Lacy (the woman who had invited Ramona to her first meeting), if it hadn't been for "the sisters," she would not have made it through.

Ramona went to one meeting, loved it, and had been spending most of her spare time interacting with the sisters in one way or another. She told me that she knew I could benefit from becoming a member of the group.

I never heard my sister speak with so much animation; therefore, I became suspicious. My sister parked her Mustang on the curb in front of a well-lit house with a beautifully manicured lawn. We both got out, and Ramona opened the back door and took out the tray of brownies that she had prepared.

Once inside the house, Ramona introduced me to the nine women who were already there, including the hostess, Janie. A buffet in the corner was crowded with sweets and appetizers. The house was spotless. The furniture was dated but well cared for. It seemed *uncultish* enough, so I helped myself to one of Ramona's brownies, a couple of cheese sticks, and some meatballs before finding a seat in the corner.

Two more women joined the group, and soon everyone was laughing and eating and laughing and eating and eating and eating and eating. They fed for about forty minutes before Janie, the hostess, called the meeting to order.

"Before we introduce our guest, let's give thanks to our Lord and Savior Jesus Christ." We bowed our heads obediently as she started to pray, "Dear Lord, thank you for allowing us the opportunity to meet and fellowship in your name. Thank you for the food that we have shared, and thank you, Lord, for the blessing you have bestowed on the women gathered in this room, and thank you *right now,* Lord, for the deliverance from earthly troubles that is promised. Amen." Now, I wasn't exactly sure what that last "thank you" meant, but I said amen anyway.

After the "amens" had died down, Janie looked at me. "Fiona, tell us a little about yourself. How long have you been divorced? How did you hear about our group?"

I stood up and circled the room with my smile before speaking. "I'm Fiona Daniels, and I'm here because my sister, Ramona, invited me." I smiled toward Ramona, who was sitting across from me. "I've been divorced for three or four months now, but we separated about a year prior to our divorce. I'm a lawyer, and it's good to meet all of you." I circled the room once more with my smile and sat back down. The sisters started asking me personal questions . . . everything from where was my church home to why did my marriage break up. I answered the questions as completely as I could while being deliberately vague. I wasn't trying to get into their sorority, so I didn't see the point of an in-depth interview.

I could tell that some of the sisters were frustrated by my answers, but I continued to circle the room with my smile. Janie ended the interrogation. She asked the other sisters to share their motto with me. The ladies, including my sister, stood up and in unison recited, *"We are divorced sisters, but we are not divorced from Christ. If we take it day by day, he will make everything right."* I hate to admit it, but the chant did seem to be a little *cultish.*

The women took their seats and the *real* meeting started. A timid-looking lady named Paulette was the first to speak. I could tell that she was trying to be strong because she had to take a deep breath before she started speaking. "Well, as you all know, I've continued to have problems with my ex-husband. He's not paying support like he's supposed to, but that's okay, because I just got a big raise at work." There was a chorus of "amens" and "praise Gods." "He just won't leave me alone. He calls me all times of night, he drives by my house, and he won't bring the children home when he's supposed to. I'm really scared he might do something crazy."

I was about to suggest a restraining order when Lacy, the woman who had introduced Ramona to the group, asked that we all bow our heads. She led us in what I thought was a less than touching prayer. "Dear Lord, continue to watch over and bless Paulette and her children. Thank you for the recent increase that she has seen at her job. Lord, we know that your word says 'ask and it shall be given,' we come to you right now, Lord, asking that you remove the demon known as Luther from her life by death or any means you see fit."

By *death* or any means . . . Damn! I would have gone for the restraining order, but maybe that's the lawyer in me. The prayer went on for another thirty to forty-five seconds, but I didn't hear anything after the death wish. Paulette thanked the women for their well wishes, and I have to admit she did look more empowered than she had before the prayer.

The next woman to take center stage was Taiwan. She was a fierce-looking woman with perfectly arched eyebrows and the best looking French manicure I had ever seen. I made a mental note to myself to find out the name of her salon before we left. She told us that she had been hiding the fact that she was seeing a high school janitor from her *engineer* ex-husband. "It ain't none of his damn business," came from one of the women.

Taiwan entertained us with the story of her last meeting with her ex-husband. She and her *janitor* friend ran into him and his *female* companion in the lobby of a movie theater. I like to have a full picture when I'm hearing a story, so I interrupted politely to ask what his female was wearing. Her look told me that the question was irrelevant to the story and that I would be wasting my time asking for the name of her salon.

Anyway, everyone was introduced, and the men shook hands. Her ex-husband asked the janitor what he did for a living, and the janitor said, "I'm a janitor". Taiwan said it pissed her off that he (her ex) had the nerve to get into her personal business like that. But in my opinion, he did what a lot of men would have done in that situation. Nothing irks a man more than for his ex to end up with someone with more money (see the coming exception).

The ex called Taiwan the next week smirking and reminding her that he told her that she would regret leaving him because it was not easy to find a man with his credentials. *Now here comes the good part of the story.* Taiwan said that she smirked right back into the phone and said, "Yeah, you're right, he doesn't make a lot of money, but his dick is huge." *Exception: Bigger dick trumps bigger salary.* Taiwan said that immediately after hanging up the phone, she begged the Lord's forgiveness for being so vulgar. The other sisters assured her that it had been necessary.

There were many more such stories. By the end of the night, I had a bad taste in my mouth;

I wasn't sure if it was because of the cleansing bitter green tea that our hostess served us right before the final prayer, or because some of the bitterness that spewed so powerfully from the women had slipped past my lips and into my mouth. I was ready to leave.

Ramona looked at me expectantly as she was pulling away from the curb. "Well, what do you think? Are you interested in coming back?"

I took a deep breath and decided to tell her the truth. "I don't want to offend you, Ramona, but I didn't like it. I don't think that it serves any good purpose for a bunch of women to get together several times a week for the sole purpose of bitching about their ex-husbands." *A couple of times a year is all that I allow myself.* Of course, she took offense.

"That's not what we do!" she shouted across the seat at me. "We support one another. Some of us *nonlawyers* don't have thousands of dollars to spend on therapy." *Yeah, but they have hundreds of dollars to spend on dessert.*

"Don't shout at me," I instructed her calmly. "You asked me what I thought and I told you. You do what you want to do, but I'm not about to start spending all of my spare time with a bunch of Christian women—and I'm using the term loosely—who curse like sailors and use cheesecake like Band-Aids." Ramona shook her head from side to side. I could feel balls of anger and hurt bouncing off the windows of the Mustang.

"That's so typical of you, Fee. If you don't approve of something, then it's not worthwhile. Participating in the group has been a positive experience for me. Maybe you haven't noticed, because you're so fucking determined to be the "gay divorcée," but it's hard for some of us.

"I've been depressed, not interested in doing much of anything . . . mad all the time. I'm scared and I'm alone. I can't keep living like this."

Actually, Ramona had always been like that; but if she wanted to blame her *naturally* sour personality on a failed marriage, I wasn't going to argue with her, especially when I saw a tear slide down her cheek. I had never seen my sister cry. I racked my brain for something positive to say. "Well, what about that guy you were seeing when I had my divorce party?" Too late I remembered what my mom had said about "the guy."

"What guy? Oh, that guy . . . It didn't work out." There was a short awkward silence before Ramona continued pouring her heart out. "I don't know what to do anymore, Fee. I go to work, I go home, I eat, sleep, and the same thing happens the next day. I don't have any real friends. Maybe the group is not the answer, but I'm tired of crying over the same old thing. I can't do this anymore," she said again. A sob escaped her and she put her fist to her forehead and leaned forward in her seat.

I felt a lump in *my* throat. Damn! We had our issues, but I loved my sister tremendously. I didn't like to see her in so much pain. I also didn't like to see her slumped over the steering wheel traveling fifty miles an hour with me in the passenger seat. So after insisting that she pull over, I took her in my arms for a fierce hug. She hugged me back and cried for a while.

My sister was in trouble, and it seemed as if she needed my help. I let her cry, and I noticed, but didn't flinch, when something that felt very much like nose drainage ran down my bare shoulder. After a while I pushed her away from me but held on to her shoulders. The street-lights allowed me to see her face clearly, and I hoped that she could see and feel my sincerity.

"Ramona, I know we don't get along some-times. Never . . . we have never gotten along," I admitted. "But *I'm* your friend, and I love you. You're a beautiful woman." And she really was, despite the fact that her hairstyle was outdated and she dressed like she was always on her way to or had just come back from a funeral.

"If you're lonely, hanging out with a bunch of other lonely women is not going to fix that. Get out . . . make your own opportunities. Do what *you* want to do for the first time in your life. I know that Pierce didn't treat you right, but you're supposed to live well and pray a little prayer that he rots in hell." Pierce was her ex-husband. Ramona laughed a sorry laugh and wiped some of the slobber from her cheeks, but not from my shoulder.

"We can't always do what we want to do, Fee. There's a little thing called consequences." I couldn't imagine anything that my sister would want to do that she would have to be concerned about the consequences.

"Listen, if it's good for you, give yourself per-mission to say to hell with the consequences." Ramona reached over and took a napkin from her glove compartment and handed it to me. She had noticed my shoulder.

"That's more you than me, Fee."

"That's true, but look at it this way, if you continue doing what you're doing, you're going to *stay* miserable. Try my way and see how you feel." Ramona and I looked at each other while I cleaned my shoulder. I am an excellent reader of expressions, and her expression told me that more than likely there was something that she would like to do.

"Okay" was all she said before she drove back onto the road. I sat back in my seat, more than a little pleased with myself. I had accomplished my mama's mission. We drove in silence and I could tell that Ramona was considering our conversation. Before I got out of the car, she grabbed my hand and squeezed it. "I love you, too, Fiona."

CHAPTER 13

I spent the next two evenings helping Ramona with an Oprah-style makeover. She got a new haircut, new makeup, a partial wardrobe, I even insisted that she trade her beat-up old wallet for something that she could be proud to take out of her new Fendi bag. I had never had so much fun with my sister.

We were nothing but positive, in other words, we had an unspoken agreement not to mention our ex-holes. Ramona's divorce had been really nasty; it involved a public official in the town where she used to live. I would tell you all about it, but I don't have the time, plus, it's not your business.

By the end of our second night together (third if you count the SCRWD meeting) Ramona looked like a woman who you wouldn't want your man to be sitting next to in a bar. She looked great. I couldn't wait for my parents to see her.

She treated me to dinner to thank me for the

encouraging words and for allowing her the benefit of my excellent taste. I wouldn't say we had a *great* time that night, but when she hugged me just before she climbed into her Mustang, it didn't feel awkward.

I was smiling to myself as I walked to my truck. "Excuse me." I turned around to face the masculine voice behind me. I figured he was talking to me because he was walking toward me and there was no one else around.

"Yes?" I held on tight to my bag, and I turned my keys in my hand so that the can of mace my father had given me was more accessible. I didn't leave because he was very good looking. He had a long, slim swimmer's body, curly hair, and a wide grin.

"I saw you leaving the restaurant with your friend and I felt like I had to introduce myself." He stepped a little closer and held his hand out like he wanted me to kiss it. I picked up two or three of his fingers and moved them up and down, simulating a handshake.

His curly hair was a sandy brown shade, and his skin was the color of an overripe banana— an interesting and exotic combination. Years ago, I wouldn't have looked twice at a guy with a slim swimmer's body and sandy brown hair. In my former life, I had a very definite physical preference, but now I know that as long as they have good hygiene and the *basic* equipment, they're all the same when the lights go out.

I shrugged my shoulder but kept my trigger finger close to the mace. "So introduce yourself."

"Dr. Holden Branch at your service." He did

another strange thing with his hands. He made three fast circles in the air . . . I guess you could call it a flourish. I smiled, not because I was charmed, but because his theatrics amused me. After a short conversation, I gave him my cell number, because the hand that he had circled in the air was *huge*.

The next day, my cell rang at about six o'clock just as I was walking out of my office. I didn't recognize the number, so I let it ring and checked for a message when I got to the parking garage. "Hi, Fiona, this is Dr. Branch . . . Holden; we met last night. I was hoping that we could meet for a drink tonight or tomorrow if you're not busy. Hit me back on my cell."

I was in no hurry to get home, so I called him back a few minutes later and agreed to meet him at a bar and grill about thirty minutes away from my office. I got there in twenty minutes and went inside to freshen up.

Dr. Branch was standing near the front entrance when I came out of the ladies' room. He saw me and started walking toward me with a wide grin on his face. There was no grin on my face. He was wearing blue scrubs, and a surgical mask rested under his chin. His gym shoes were covered in clear plastic Jheri curl bags, and he was carrying a big black leather bag.

The bag slapped me on the ass when he pulled me into his arms for a hug. Mind you, I didn't know this man. "Hey, girl. Forgive my appearance, but I'm just out of surgery." Hey, girl? Nicole calls me hey girl. I'm not going to even comment on the "just out of surgery" statement.

If it was Halloween and we were at a costume party, I would have been amused. But since we were at an upscale bar and people were starting to stare at him, I suggested that I wait at the bar while he changed. I looked pointedly at his black bag. He laughed a fake hardy laugh and lifted the black bag.

"This is my surgical bag. I carry my instruments in here. They're very expensive, so I didn't want to leave the bag in the car. Let's grab those stools before someone else does." He walked ahead of me to the bar, and the plastic bags on his feet made squishy sounds on the hardwood floor.

I ordered a cosmopolitan, and he ordered a Shirley Temple. "I'm on call," he explained.

"Oh, really?" I could hardly open my mouth to comment. I watched as the bartender poured my drink into a martini glass. "Dr." Branch looked ridiculous sipping his drink from the stirrer, but since I knew I would be on my way home in less than twenty minutes, I didn't care.

"What hospital are you affiliated with?" I asked for the hell of it.

"All of them," he said without batting an eye. Then, I swear to God, he proceeded to tell me that he was a heart transplantologist . . . *a heart transplantologist!* He showed me a pager and said that whenever "they" had a heart come in, "they" paged him and he would usually meet the helicopter on the roof of the hospital. After he "put the heart in," "they" would pay him *cash on the spot*. That way, he said, he was able to work with all of the hospitals around town, he didn't have to worry about leasing office space, and he didn't have to pay taxes.

I'm telling you he sat on the cherry wood bar stool with the green leather seat and told me that story. He was crazy. I knew he was crazy, because as I have previously mentioned, I am an excellent reader of expressions. I could tell by the expression on his face that he believed the ridiculous bullshit that came out of his mouth.

I didn't say anything until I finished my drink; then I turned to him with an equally straight face. "Sounds like very challenging work." I looked down at my watch. "I wish I could stay for another drink, but I'm from out of town . . . Pluto, to be precise. My commanding officer has just summoned me back to the spacecraft. It was nice meeting you, Earthling, but my time on your planet is over." I grabbed my purse and walked robotically out of the bar, squealing like an alien pig for added effect.

I was laughing so hard that I had to pull over about an eighth of a mile down the road. I called Nicole on my cell to tell her about my adventure. After we finished laughing, she chastised me as if I were the child that she longed to have.

"You're going to get enough of going out with people you don't know. Do you think he had money to pay for the drinks?"

"Girl, I don't know and I don't care. I just pray that he figures that Pluto is out of range and doesn't try to call my cell phone again." We laughed some more. Nicole continued talking as I got back on the road.

"I have to go. I'm making dinner for *my* doctor . . . who will be home any minute. Hey, don't forget about my cousin. He should call you tomorrow or the next night."

"Didn't you just tell me I shouldn't go out with people I don't know?"

"*I* know him, and you better treat him right." After our conversation ended, I decided to call my sister and tell her about my thirteen-minute adventure. Dialing the number made me feel good. It was the first time that I had ever thought to share anything funny with her.

CHAPTER 14

I agreed to meet Nicole's cousin on Saturday after dinner with my parents. My parents couldn't get over the remarkable change in Ramona's appearance. My mom took me aside before we sat down to eat and kissed me on both cheeks. "Is she out of that cult?"

I was happy that she was happy. "I really don't think it's a cult, but I don't think she's going to any more meetings."

"Thank you, honey. I could hardly enjoy my vacation from worrying about your sister. You should have called me right away to let me know that you had fixed everything." She gave me the "you know better" eye.

I didn't take offense at what most people would have considered a lack of real appreciation . . . with my mother, praise and condemnation went hand in hand. Ramona was whining from across the room that she was ready to eat . . . "fixed everything" was a definite overstatement.

We sat down to cabbage, sweet and sour pig's

feet, turkey necks, homemade corn bread, and yams. *Don't tell nobody, but Fiona love huh some pig's feet.* Ramona does, too, but she reported to us that she was thinking about giving up red meat. She piled her plate high with the "more easily digested," more sophisticated turkey necks.

After dinner I showered and changed at my parent's house. I put on a shimmery green summer dress. It was sexy, but not so sexy that my father tried to send me back up to my old room to change when I said good-bye.

Samuel and I had agreed to meet at The Maze, a well-established nightspot for the 25 and over crowd for drinks and dancing. I called him on his cell when I was ten minutes away from the club. He was already there but said that he would come out to meet me.

I added more gloss to my lips and fluffed my hair before I stepped out of my truck. A vaguely familiar–looking *big . . . tall . . . fine* man was standing near the entrance of the club. My fingers crossed automatically in my head. *Please let this be him.*

"Fee?" It was the voice that I had heard on the phone. He sounded as if he should be a dj on an all-request love line. Before I finished nodding my head, he scooped me up for a combination hug/twirl. He felt good, and he smelt good . . . I mean *smelled* good, too. "Damn, girl, you grew up. You were always pretty, but if I had known you were going to turn into a certified honey, I would have stayed in the Carolinas." I smiled at him. I was not immune to flattery . . . especially from a semichildhood friend.

He was grinning to the back of his ears when he put me down. I liked him immediately, or at least I liked his *looks*. He wore chocolate-colored linen slacks and a button-down shirt in a lighter shade of the same expensive-looking linen. Leather sandals exposed his clean masculine toes.

"Be glad you didn't stay, because it looks like California has been good to you." I even liked the modest way he nodded his head.

"Let's go in and get this party started!" He took my hand and pulled me behind him. Normally his action would have upset me, but I was happy for the excellent view of his ass.

We caught up over our first two drinks. He knew that I was divorced. He had never married, but he had been *engaged* three times. There was a story there, but it had nothing to do with me, and he had too many "goods" going on for me to be concerned about it. He had made a *good* life for himself, he was *good* looking, he had a *good* sense of humor, and best of all, he lived a *good* 2500 miles away from me. And I was pretty sure his pockets were as deep as his voice. Nicole had hooked a sista up!

The two of us made a party. The conversation never lagged, and he was an excellent dancer. He was fun. I was even impressed that he said no to a fourth drink.

We left the club after about three hours. He held my hand as he escorted me to my truck. "Thank you for coming out to see me. If not for you I would have been stuck in my hotel running up an outrageous pay-per-view bill. You saved me."

"Anytime, sir." Of course, he leaned in to kiss me, and of course, I was ready. And he was a *good* kisser. We kissed good together. He stroked his hand against the sensitive skin on the side of my neck. The invitation was offered casually.

"My hotel is not far from here. Sometimes there are some good movies on pay-per-view. You interested?"

"Are you trying to get me back to your hotel?"

"I wouldn't respect myself if I didn't try." He kissed me again, but this time the kiss was a deep promise. When the kiss was over, it took me a second to open my eyes. I said yes because I was curious to know what his hands would feel like under the silk of my dress.

His hotel room was nice . . . very expensive looking. But I wasn't interested in the view or the room rate. Samuel broke open the minibar and made us both a rum and coke. Most of the movies on pay-per-view were soft porn . . . at least the ones that caught my eye. Just between you and me, I prefer my porn a little hard core, but that didn't stop me from settling down to watch *Desert Heat* with my new old friend.

It was a "torrid tale" about a group of ranger looking people who get stranded in an unnamed desert. I don't know why they were in the desert, or how they'd gotten lost, but luckily, one of the rangers thought to pack strawberries, whipped cream, body oil, and condoms along with his compass.

There were three men and five women, and every one of the five women wore thongs and lacy bras under their Daisy Duke khakis. They scouted the arid land until they happened upon a natural Jacuzzi. I'm sure you know what happens next, *don't pretend like you don't.*

Samuel and I laughed and made crazy observations throughout most of the movie, but by the time Ranger C had Ranger A in a . . . Well, you'll just have to rent the movie to find out why his hand was on my . . . Just rent the movie!

I put my hand on his thigh and he moved his hand up to massage my neck. I rolled my head around like women do to encourage a man to keep going. "That feels good." That short statement was all the prompting that he needed. I don't know what happened to his hands, but he started caressing the side of my neck with his mouth. His lips were moist, but dry like I like. When he put the tip of his tongue in my ear, I got that feeling that a woman gets when she knows that something good is about to happen.

He was an expert kisser, and I fully enjoyed the feel of his lips and tongue. He pushed the thin straps of my dress down and kissed and bit into my shoulders. I moved my hands up to unbutton his shirt. He didn't have a six-pack, but his skin was hard with some definition.

My hand moved down from his chest, but he pushed me on my back before I found my target. He straddled me and moved to unbuckle his pants. We hadn't talked about going *there*, but I was willing. I sat back up and took the job from him. I slid his pants down over his hips, and with as much boldness as I had ever shown, put both hands in his white cotton underwear.

"That's right, baby," he moaned. I had to move my hands up a little, then up a little more. That's when things started to get uncomfortable. I moved my hands up a little more and discovered, to put it delicately, the object of my desire left much to be desired. In not so delicate terms, *fully* erect—and I mean as hard as a diamond— his dick was about half as long as a bun-length hot dog, with about the same girth as said hot dog. I had heard the term *needle dick* before, but I swear, I had never encountered one.

I stoked him a few more times to make sure that I wasn't mistaken. He moaned again. "Careful, Fiona, I'm about to explode." *Needle dick and possibly a premature ejaculator . . . no . . . no . . . no! I'm not saying that I would* never *screw a man with a tiny dick . . . well, actually I am saying that.*

I pulled my hands out of his shorts. I had to think fast. What to do? What to say? He moved until his body was resting on top of mine and started kissing the side of my neck again. "Let's take this to the bed," he suggested. I moaned and started pushing gently but firmly against him. "What is it?"

I was very apologetic. Shit, I was as sorry as hell! "I can't do this. I thought I could, but my divorce is so fresh that I really can't handle a physical encounter right now. My emotions are too close to the surface." It was a lie of course, but he didn't know that. "I'm so sorry, Samuel, I shouldn't have let things get this far."

He offered no resistance as I struggled to get

up. When we were sitting side by side on the sofa he took my hand in his and started to kiss and nibble on my fingers. It felt good, and I couldn't stop the moan that slipped past my lips. "Are you sure?" he asked. I nodded and put my hand in my lap. He was not ready to give up. Samuel took my head in his hand and kissed me very sweetly on the mouth. He put his lips against my ear.

"I have more than one weapon in my arsenal. Let me lick you, Fiona; I promise you won't be sorry." The request was rather abrupt, but damn, it was tempting! As his tongue trailed from my ear to my neck, it occurred to me that he probably knew that he had a little dick, it may have had a little something (no pun intended) to do with his three broken engagements.

If I was a selfish woman, I would have taken him up on his offer. But because I am so very unselfish, if I allowed him to do *me* I would feel obliged to do *him*. I just couldn't wrap my mind *or* my lips around that. So I grabbed my purse and my shoes and brought a quick end to the most uncomfortable date I had ever had.

When I got home I undressed and reached into my little silver toy box for something to help me finish what Samuel had started. I took out the smallest vibrator I owned, and in memory of the night's thwarted festivities named it Samuel . . . big Samuel. I drifted off to sleep with the image of Nick in my head. Now *Nick* . . . Nick had a big dick.

CHAPTER 15

I know I've been rambling, but I just want you to know why I ended up speaking to Nick again after the whole "I disapprove of your dress" fiasco. My intention was never to speak to him again. Regardless of the size of his phallus and his mastery of creamy sauces, I knew I didn't want to spend time with any man who wanted to change anything about me.

I had made up my mind months ago that I would never change anything for a man—not my phone number, not my opinion, not my routine, and certainly not my fashion sense. And technically, I stuck to that resolve. I didn't change my mind because of Nick; I changed it because it was what *I* wanted to do . . . and plus, he caught me at a weak moment.

Exactly fourteen days after my last meeting with Nick, I was going over some notes for a case outside the courtroom when I heard a chillingly familiar voice calling my name. "Fiona!" My hands froze; then I slipped the notecards in the side of my briefcase. I took mental inventory of my appearance—beautifully tailored suit, new pumps, tasteful jewelry, my favorite Bobbi Brown lipstick—I looked good enough to appear before the Supreme Court.

I turned around slowly to face my ex-hole. I hadn't seen or spoken to him since our last appearance in court. You'd think that since we were both lawyers that we would have run into one another sooner, but as luck or God would have it, we hadn't. My expression was cool and professional, but my eyebrow arch said, *What the fuck do you want?* No, it said, *What the fuck is your problem?* No *no*, it said, *I'll fuck you up!*

I looked him up and down. Most of you are probably curious to know what he looks likes. It's not relevant to the story, but *just* to satisfy your curiosity . . .

He looked about the same, except he had mucus oozing from the corners of his eyes. Big yellow dandruff flakes were in his beard, and his black nails were filed to a point. Thorns had replaced the hair on his head, and his eyes were bloodshot. Oh, and he had a long, thin tail growing out of the hole in his ass. *Well, that's what he looks like to me.* Frankly, I was surprised they allowed him in court looking and smelling the way that he did.

"Fiona, I thought that was you. How are you doing?" Oh, my God, he had the audacity to try and sound friendly. I didn't *say* anything, I let my eyebrow do the talking. The following is a play in one act featuring my eyebrow and my ex-hole.

THE BEAUTY AND THE BASTARD
by
Me, Myself, and I

EYEBROW: Fuck you fuck you fuck you!

EX-HOLE: You look good.

EYEBROW: I look fucking great and you know it.

EX-HOLE: Don't be like that, Fee.

EYEBROW: Like what? You fucking whore-monger.

EX-HOLE: Fine, then, I'll talk. Obviously, you're still hurt and angry, but I want you to know that I'm not the same old Wilson. I'm going to church, I'm a vegetarian . . .

EYEBROW: *(refusing to listen to his bullshit)* I don't give a fuck!

EX-HOLE: *(sighing like the bitch that he is)* Okay, Fee, I have to get to a meeting back at my office, but we really need to talk. We need closure, and there are some things that are going on in my life right now that I really need to talk to you about; the sooner the better. Please call me.

FIONA, STANDING IN FOR EYEBROW: *(polite smile pasted on her face)* There is noth-

ing that we need to discuss. In the future,
if our paths happen to cross, I would prefer it if you didn't speak to me, but if you
must, please call me Fiona. Don't call me
Fee . . . don't evah call me Fee. I only allow
my family and friends to call me Fee, and
we both know how you fucked up that
privilege.

*Fiona exits; hoping the image of her perfect,
round ass will be burned into his mind forever.
She does not exhale until she enters the courtroom.*

THE END

Two hours later, after having lost my client's
bid to gain controlling interest of her family's
pig farm (long story), I left the courthouse. I
hated losing. Running into my ex-hole had cost
me my case. I could hardly focus on what was
going on around me, because I was so busy
thinking of other things that I coulda/ shoulda
said with my eyebrows.

My cell phone rang just as I had figured out
how to arch my eyebrow into *damn you.* It was
Nick. I answered because I needed someone to
be rude to. "What?" I barked into the phone.

"Where's my money?"

The question caught me off guard. "What
money?"

"The last time I saw you I handed you a hundred dollars. It was a loan, not a gift." His tone
was smooth and pleasant like it normally was, so
I was *pretty* sure he was kidding, but with men
you never knew.

"Your son ruined my dress. You owe *me* money."

"So keep the fifteen dollars that you paid for the dress and bring the change to my house on Sunday." He laughed into the phone. I smiled, myself but I didn't let him know it.

"Ha *ha,* you're so funny . . . so funny I forgot to laugh."

He laughed for me or *at* me. "Now *that's* funny; I haven't heard that expression since the sixth grade. Okay, you can keep the money, but come to my house on Sunday. I'll barbeque for you." I didn't say anything. "Come on, Fee, I miss your nasty attitude." *Fee? Who gave him permission to call me Fee?*

"I don't eat barbeque," I lied.

"Yes, you do, I've seen you eat barbeque. I've seen you swallow a fat sausage link whole . . . *Well, that wasn't exactly barbeque.*" He laughed at his own joke. I let up a little and laughed too. I had almost forgotten how easy it was to laugh with Nick.

"You are a very vulgar individual. And anyway, who said it was a *fat* sausage link?"

"*You* did, but come over Sunday and I'll be more than happy to refresh your memory." His voice was cajoling, and I decided to relent. Nick had been serving his purpose well before the "I don't like your dress" thing. What kind of woman would I be if I let a man's bad taste in clothes stand between me and a good piece of *fat, hot sausage?*

"What time Sunday?" I asked.

"You tell me. I've decided not to go into the restaurant on Sunday's anymore. I'm letting Sandoval take care of things." Sandoval was his assistant general manager.

"I'll be there at three. I may go to church."
Nick laughed, presumably at the thought of me
going to church, but he didn't comment on it.

"You remember the address?"

"Yes, Nick, I'm not an idiot. I've been there
several times?"

"There's that nasty attitude that I like." He
laughed into the phone before hanging up. My
mood was much improved when I pushed the
red End button on my cell. To be totally honest
with you, as far as men go *(and we know how far
that is)*, Nick was awight.

CHAPTER 16

On Sunday morning, I set my alarm clock early enough for church. I pictured myself showing up at Nick's saying, "The Reverend *sho'* preached a good service this *maw*nin'." But when the alarm went off I unplugged it and turned over. I spent part of my Sunday morning in bed and part of it at the high school track not far from my home.

I went running, took a shower, returned some phone calls, and then got *back* into bed for a quick nap before putting on my barbeque gear. I paired a denim skirt with a red halter top. I wore sequined canvas sneakers instead of sandals. My outfit was very appropriate for a Sunday afternoon barbeque . . . above reproach. The halter wasn't cut very low, and the material didn't cling to my breasts. Not that I cared about what Nick thought about my outfit; I just like to dress more conservatively on Sundays. My mother was always calling at the last minute to tell me to stop by for cake or pie or something.

* * *

Nick's home was a three-bedroom, three-and-a-half-bath, efficiently designed beauty. The architect/chef himself had drawn up the plans and had overseen the construction. The exterior of the house was a stark white. The landscaping was lush but simple. The first time I'd visited Nick at home, the fact that everything whispered high design, from the front door to the Philippe Starck bathroom fixtures, had not been lost on me.

I rang the bell and waited with an indifferent smile on my face for Nick to answer . My smile faltered when Noelle, his daughter, opened the door. Her smile was as indifferent as mine had been. She looked me up and down and said, "Cool shoes." She held the door open for me and turned around to shout, "Dad, your girlfriend's here."

"I'm *not* his girlfriend," I protested. She shrugged her shoulders.

"Whatever you say." Nick came from the direction of the kitchen, drying his hands with a paper towel. He was wearing khaki shorts and a baby blue T-shirt. "I'm finished with the beans, Dad, can I call Macy?"

"Yeah, but first let your brother know that he has lemonade detail in fifteen minutes."

"Okay." I could detect no animosity in the smile that she gave us. He handed her the paper towel as she walked past him.

"Nice shoes" was the first thing he said to me. I looked down at my sparkling shoes, then back up at him.

"Yes, they are. You didn't tell me that your kids were going to be here."

He smiled the "you amuse me" smile. "I didn't realize that I needed your permission to have my kids spend some time in *their* home."

"You know what I mean, Nick. You gave me the impression that it would just be the two of us."

"Are you saying that you were looking forward to spending some time alone with me?" I rolled my eyes in response. "There it is . . . that nasty attitude that I have come to know and love." I couldn't help but laugh, and he laughed with me. "I know what you mean, Fee, and I know that the first meeting didn't go well. But I'm a firm believer that when you fall off a horse you need to get back on. My kids are great, and though you try to hide it, you're great, too. I think we can break bread together without incident." He took my purse and placed it on the Ashanti stool in the entryway. I followed him into the kitchen.

"You should have told me," I muttered.

He turned around to face me and took me in his arms. "You're right, I should have, but I knew you probably wouldn't come if I did. Please forgive me?" He started raining tiny kisses on my forehead. My forehead is one of my five . . . no *six* . . . really erogenous zones. Nick had discovered that tidbit during the many hours of downtime that we had logged together. He covered my mouth with his and kissed me like he had really missed me. "Forgive me?" he asked again.

"I'll let you know after I eat." I extricated myself from his arms and looked around the kitchen. Fixings for a potato salad were laid out on the granite countertop. Through the glass-paneled French doors I saw a pit smoking on the deck.

"There's wine and beer in the refrigerator and a pitcher of margaritas in the freezer; help yourself," he offered.

His son walked into the kitchen just as I took the blender from the freezer. "Hi." He smiled at me like he didn't know we had problems and opened the refrigerator. "Where are the lemons, Dad?"

"Damn! I knew I forgot something." Nick looked at me and at my margarita. "Fee, would you mind holding off on that for a minute and driving Nathan to the store for some lemons. We have an unwritten rule around here that we can't have barbeque without lemonade. Nathan knows how to get to the store."

What was I supposed to say, *hell yeah, I mind.* My mama raised me better than that. "No problem," I lied. Nathan was barefoot like his dad. "Put on some shoes, and don't give Miss Fiona any problems." *Miss Fiona?* I didn't like the sound of that.

Nathan jumped in my truck like he was testing the springs in the seat for some consumer organization. He buckled his seat belt, then slammed the passenger door so hard that I cringed. "Take it easy . . . I'm still paying for this truck." *Unlike the dress that you ruined,* I thought to myself. He said sorry, but he was almost laughing when he said it.

When I started the truck, hip-hop blasted from the speakers. I liked loud music, and I usually rode solo.

Nathan covered his ears and I turned down

the volume. "That's okay; you can turn it back up. My dad likes to listen to loud music, but he only listens to jazz and some old stuff. My mom doesn't let us listen to the radio in the car. She said that we should talk to each other in the car." *Too much information.* I turned the volume back up to prohibit further conversation.

After a few minutes of driving straight ahead I turned to Nathan. "Your dad said that you knew where the store is."

"Yeah, just keep straight and turn at the third stop sign, then you'll be on the main street." Nick's neighborhood was a nice mixture of old and new. People were buying up the older houses to bulldoze them and start from scratch, or preserving the original structure and expanding and updating; that's what Nick had done.

"What is horny?" The question came from the passenger seat.

"*What?*"

"The guy in the song said, 'You make me so horny.' What is horny?" Hey, I don't *listen* to the words, I just enjoy the beat. Maybe his mom was on to something with her "no radio allowed" rule. I flipped off the radio, hoping he'd forget his question, but he asked again.

Damn! I did what my mother had done when similar situations had come up when I was a girl—I lied. "Well, sometimes when people are upset, they get so angry that they feel like horns are growing out of their heads. Then they say, 'I'm so horny'; or to another person, 'You make me so horny.' *Like your dad,* I thought to myself, *your dad makes me so horny.* I felt like a teacher. Before he could ask for more details, I changed the subject, "Your dad said that the store was nearby."

"There are lots of stores around here. Turn left at this corner." I drove for twenty minutes before we got to the store. We passed several, but Nathan insisted that his father only liked produce from one particular store . . . *just like a chef.*

The store was in a neighborhood that I wouldn't want to have a flat tire in at any time of the day. It was hard for me to imagine that they had a top-notch produce department.

"I don't think this is the right store," I told Nathan. There were five men standing on the broken concrete/sidewalk outside the store. They looked like they were on a break from shooting a rap video. One was smoking a cigarette, a couple of them were smoking something else, and one man, who was wearing a stretched-out white muscle shirt that called attention to his ripped arms and chest and his black velvet canvas–colored skin, was just plain *smoking*. I forgot about all safety concerns for a minute and just looked at him. Damn, but he was fine!

Nathan interrupted me before I lost myself in the fantasy of possibilities. "It's okay," he assured me.

"How do you know? Have you been here before?"

"No, but I've always wanted to come," he answered honestly. I looked again at the small building with the dingy bricks and the faded hand-painted sign: ATOM'S CORNER STORE.

"Why would you want to come here?"

"Because I like to look at people, and mostly I look at the same people every day. My dad says I am a social anthropologist." Since I liked to look at people, too, I turned off the engine and walked with him toward the store. The men out front turned their attention to us and watched as we approached.

We heard, "superstar," "Can I come with you?" "yeah, baby . . . move that ass," "wait a minute," and some things that I blocked out in the short seconds that it took us to actually get inside the store.

As we walked down the aisle, Nathan asked me with great sincerity, "Were those men talking to me?"

I laughed a little and put my hand on his back to hurry him on. "Let's hope not, baby, and let's hope this store actually sells produce."

Later, as we sipped our ginger lemonade, I told Nick about the conversation that Nathan and I had had about the haves and the have-nots on the way back from the store. I had discovered during dinner that his kids were not as bad as they had first appeared. They were smart and very polite to me. Nathan had apologized for my dress with much sincerity; he offered to have it cleaned. Noelle was no trouble, because she had a telephone attached to her ear for most of the afternoon. We played Scrabble, ate again, and Nick and I watched them play volleyball in the pool before it was time for them to get ready to go back to their mom's house.

CHAPTER 17

Later that evening, Nick and I were lying on his plush sheets. His kids were gone, and he had come through with the "hot sausage" like a champ. He was drifting in and out of sleep, but my mind was racing.

His ex-wife had been very polite when she came to pick up the kids. She was smiling and was 100% less uptight than she had been during our first meeting. She remembered and apologized about my dress and told me that Nathan had been ruining *her* clothes since they'd brought him home from the hospital.

Nick gave her barbeque, potato salad, and grilled fish to take home. I was waiting for them to kiss before she left. My *point* is, that day she seemed like a pretty decent woman, and their relationship did not seem to be strained or awkward. I was curious, as lawyers tend to be, so I decided a little pillow talk was in order.

"You and Yvonne seem to have a good understanding about your kids. I don't know what I would have done if kids were involved in my divorce." I waited a few seconds before getting to the question. That's what they taught us in law school: Put the defendant at ease with a compliment . . . make him think you're on his side.

"How long were you married before you divorced? Did you grow up together?" My head was resting on his chest and I was stroking his chest hairs a little, so I felt his chest move slightly when he chuckled.

"If you answer mine, I'll answer yours." I didn't want to answer any personal questions, but I knew that if I didn't he wouldn't, and like I said, I was very curious.

"Sure."

Nick adjusted my head so that he could talk more comfortably. "Yvonne and I met our freshman year at Syracuse. I was the only black man in the school of architecture at that time . . . I was out of place . . . homesick . . . horny. I decided to join the Black Student Union, and I met my ex-wife at the fall mixer. She was from New York. If she felt out of place it didn't show. She was beautiful and more sophisticated than any eighteen-year-old I have ever met. She took me under her wing and showed this country boy the ropes."

I tried to imagine Nick as a country boy, and I couldn't. "You sound like you were walking around in overalls with a toothpick in your mouth."

Nick laughed. "I don't think I was that bad, but if *Yvonne* was telling this story, she would say I was close. I mean I was a Southern boy living in upstate New York the first time. I had a lot to learn. Life got a lot better when we started dating. We were both determined to do well in school. Her family became my family . . . We fell in love.

"I took her home to my parents and they fell in love with her, too. I proposed to her when we were seniors and we got married that summer after school. We spent the first two years of our marriage in Italy—"

I interrupted him. "What for?"

"I was in a master's program and she was my wife."

"What did she do when you were in class?"

"She was taking classes at American University. She was doing her thing, and I was doing my thing. Then we moved back home, and she continued to do her own thing and vice versa. A few years into the marriage we were both ready to admit that we were unhappy, but by then we had kids. Right after Nathan was born we were arguing so much we couldn't stand to be in the same room together.

"We fought over how cool to keep the house; we fought over what kind of bread she brought home from the store. Just any stupid shit we could think of. We were arguing because we were so unhappy. And then it just *stopped*. We stopped arguing, we only talked about the kids and bills, we slept in the same room, but we weren't making love. Shit, I almost preferred the arguing.

"The marriage was just *dead*. And then Sonja came along and I just went for it."

"Sonja was the woman you had the affair with?" He was a good defendant . . . ready to spill his guts with no intense examination.

"Yeah, I guess that I had been looking for a

long time but didn't know it. This may sound crazy to you, but I thought that having a relationship with her could save my marriage."

It sounded *fucking* crazy to me, but then I'm a woman and therefore a more rational thinker. I wanted to ask him a dozen questions, and there were several things that I wanted to challenge him on, but I didn't want to interrupt his flow. I had to bide my time. I allowed him to talk some more before asking one crucial question. "What made you think that screwing another woman would help your marriage?" I felt his shoulders move.

"I don't know. Sometimes a man just needs a distraction until he can get back on track. Maybe a woman needs that too. I could talk to Sonja and not think about the fact that Yvonne and I didn't talk."

"I'm sure the two of you did a lot of talking," I said sarcastically. I was *trying*, but I had a definite bias against adulterers.

"I'm not going to tell you anything else, Fee, if you're just asking to pass judgment." He sounded irritated.

"You're right, I'm listening." *I'll just pass judgment silently, like I usually do.*

"For your information, by the time Sonja and I shared our first kiss, Yvonne and I hadn't touched each other, *not even for a kiss*, in eight months."

How sweet, they shared their first kiss. Poor baby, Nick . . . at least he had a real legitimate reason for screwing around.

"And I'm not going to lie." I'm sure I've already mentioned that Nick is against lying . . .

unless there's a wife involved. Bada boom . . . okay, no more I can't stand a lying, cheating, bastard one-liners. "Making love with someone different after so many years was refreshing."

Refreshing? Is that what the kids are calling it? I continued my silent game. He was silent after that, so I felt it was appropriate to ask another question.

"How did she find out?"

"I told her," he said simply. He *told* her . . . even *I* knew that was stupid. "I told her because I was ashamed of myself. I felt like I was using Sonja, and I knew in my heart that I didn't want Yvonne anymore."

"So she left you?"

He shifted his weight again. "No . . . Damn, can I just tell the story?" His tone was rough but playful. "I told her because I knew I had to leave. We weren't living a married life, and I'd had enough. She didn't want me to leave. She wanted us to go to counseling. She talked about the kids and about dividing wealth, but she didn't want to talk about us. She didn't want me either, but she was satisfied with the status quo.

"When I left, I didn't know that I wasn't coming back." He hesitated for a minute before continuing, "And about my kids . . . the biggest regret that I have is that they won't have the experience that I had growing up. They won't grow up seeing their mother and father together, knowing that they love one another . . . having Thanksgiving and Christmas in one house . . . Hell, I'm even going to have to split time with my grandchildren when they come."

His concern for his kids touched me enough

to stop the silent recriminations I mean, I could have thought something like, *well, you should have thought about that before you decided to drop your designer slacks*, but I didn't.

"When a marriage breaks up it's hard . . . especially hard when children are involved. After my parents died, I thought about asking her to give us another chance. We were already divorced, but they were the only family I had. I didn't ask her, because after all was said and done, I still felt like we couldn't live our best lives together. I still don't know if doing what I felt was in my best interest was what was best for my children."

Okay, his sincerity really touched me this time. I believed that he was sincere because I had witnessed firsthand his relationship with his children and how important they were to him. I could feel his heart beating against my cheek. It was beating slower . . . I imagined it was from regret.

"If you had to do it again, would you?"

"No, I would have lived the life I signed up for." Nick took a deep breath, and I felt like he wanted to say something else, but he didn't. He allowed the heavy silence to stay in the room to the point that I was beginning to feel uncomfortable before he asked his question.

"So tell me your divorce story."

Fair is fair, so I didn't hesitate, but in the end I said more than I intended to. "One day I had a husband who would rub my back at night and tell me the next morning he was tired because he had spent part of the night just watching me sleep. We laughed together. He smiled at me and told me how beautiful I was. We spent time every week wondering what I would look like pregnant. He told me that he couldn't imagine life without me and that I was the only woman for him. I thought we were happy.

"And the next day I found out that the same husband who was watching me sleep and promising me babies was screwing his hired help. Like I said, I honestly thought we were happy. I wish I could tell you that we *were* having major problems, or that he was on crack or something, because maybe then I could understand and explain it to you better. For me, it would have been better if he had said, 'Fee, I just don't like you.'

"It's scary to put your trust in someone . . . to think that you know them, and then discover that they're living a lie, and therefore, so are you."

"So you didn't have any clue?"

I laughed briefly before answering his question. "I had a lot of clues, but I didn't know at the time they were clues. He was so romantic and so believable that he could dismiss any concern that I had to my satisfaction. When I think about the amount of shit I let him feed me . . . it's scary.

"But what's even scarier than that is the fact that five minutes after I found out, I didn't love him anymore. And I had to wonder if I had ever loved him at all." I was surprised at the emotions that I felt telling him my story. Nick stroked my hair.

"You had to shut off your feelings to get through a hard time."

I moved my body away from him and sat up

with my back against the headboard. "No . . . can I tell *my* story, please?" We smiled at each other in the dim light before I continued. "It was stranger than that. It wasn't me *pretending* not to love him because he hurt me. When I read through those first e-mails, I just knew almost instantly that I didn't love him anymore and that our marriage was over." He interrupted me again. "So that's how you found out . . . You read his personal e-mails?" I detected a note of disapproval in his voice.

"*Yes . . . I . . . did.*"

"You just told me that you weren't having any marital problems. Why would you read his e-mails?" He was about to piss me off.

"Are you trying to cross-examine me? I told you we weren't having any major problems, and we weren't. I was using his laptop one evening, and I don't know whether it was the devil or God's divine intervention that made me go to his e-mail. The e-mails looked pretty normal, but then I checked to see what was in his trash. He hadn't emptied his trash in weeks, and there I found all I never wanted to know."

"Do you think it was right for you to go through his personal things?"

"Nick, get over the e-mail thing. . . . I did it and I'm glad I did. Me infringing on his right to privacy is not relevant in this conversation. And you focusing on *that* instead of the havoc and devastation that he wrecked in my life is a typical male response." I was officially pissed off, and I was about to throw the covers off my lap and take my ass home, but he held my arm and apologized.

"You're right, Fee . . . It's not relevant. Please continue."

"I was just trying to say that the whole experience made me realize that I don't know what love is. I don't know what love between a man and a woman is supposed to be. I'm not even curious about it anymore."

Nick was quiet. I was beginning to think that he had dozed off, but then he spoke. "Haven't your parents been married for years? You have a live model to refer to."

"Yeah, they've been married for years, but they never let me and my sister see much of their relationship. I don't know what has kept them together and sane all these years, and I'm taking liberties with the term *sane*."

"Are you saying that your experience has made you give up on love?"

I thought for a minute before answering his question. "No, I wouldn't say that I've given up on love. I would say that my experience with love is like my experience with smoking: I tried it once, but it left a very bad taste in my mouth. It was my first and last cigarette."

Nick was quiet again, but I knew he wasn't sleeping. I didn't want to discuss my divorce story anymore, and I didn't want him to make any comments. I sat up straighter in the bed. I sounded abrupt to myself. "It's late. I have to get going."

He pulled me back down to his chest playfully. "You're not going anywhere."

"I have to go to work tomorrow." I looked at the clock on his nightstand. Technically, it was already tomorrow.

"Tomorrow is a holiday." It was the Fourth of July. I kissed the underside of his jaw. I don't know why I did that.

"Lawyers are like restaurateurs," I muttered against his late-night stubble, "holidays can be very busy for us." I sat up again and he pulled me back down. I giggled, a real *schoolgirl* giggle.

"Well, go in late then."

I started to get up again, but his sheets were so soft. The thread count was probably 500. I *could* go in late tomorrow . . . hell, I could work from home . . . it was too late for me to drive across town . . . drunk drivers come out in droves on holiday weekends . . . I was sleepy . . . he would make me breakfast if I stayed . . . make love to me again in the morning . . . his sheets were *so* soft.

CHAPTER 18

Nick and I kinda fell into a different understanding after that night at his house. Even when his son took the definition of "horny" that I gave him to school and was suspended for a day for telling his male math teacher, "You make me so horny," there were no major waves.

The boy's mom was upset, but I wasn't sleeping with her, and she wasn't buying me dinner two or three times a week. So as my mom would say, to hell with her. My mom would actually say *fuck her*, but I'm being polite.

No, wait a minute! I need to back up. It was about three or four Sundays *after* the barbeque when things kinda shifted for us.

Nick and I had been to an early afternoon concert in the park, and he was going to drop me off at home (my home), then pick up his kids. I asked him to stop at my favorite frozen yogurt shop on the way home. I stayed in the car while he went inside to get our yogurts.

You don't know this about me, but I try not to

ask for much. So when I *do* ask for something, it's because it's what I *want*—a faithful husband, a raise, respect, a particular *flavor of frozen yogurt.* I asked Nick to bring me a coconut frozen yogurt in a waffle cone . . . a coconut frozen yogurt in a waffle cone.

He handed me the cone when he got back into the car. Nick put his shake into the cup holder and backed up the car. I sampled my yogurt and frowned. "This doesn't taste like coconut." Nick was concentrating on getting the car on the road, so he didn't comment.

I took another lick, but this time I smacked the yogurt around in my mouth trying harder to discern a coconutty flavor. "This doesn't taste like coconut," I said again louder. Nick kept his eyes on the road. At that point I knew he was ignoring me.

"Nick!" I almost shouted . . . well, actually, I did shout. "Is this coconut yogurt?"

He turned his head to look at me. "They were out of coconut so I got you vanilla." He sounded patronizing. My lips were not in the happy formation.

"Why didn't you come back to the car and tell me they didn't have coconut? Or why didn't you say, 'Fiona, they didn't have the flavor you wanted, so I got vanilla instead.'" He sighed and shook his head . . . *like I had done something wrong.*

"Because I didn't think it was a big deal. I've seen you eat vanilla ice cream before, vanilla wafers, you drink French vanilla cappuccino . . ." Nick can really be a smart-ass.

"I *assumed* that you like vanilla." I rolled my

eyes at him. "That's not the point. You should have asked me, and you certainly should have said something when I mentioned that it didn't taste like coconut." At that point, I was rolling my head and Nick was shaking his again.

"Fiona, if you don't like it, don't eat it." I *didn't* like it, and I wasn't about to eat it. I pressed the button to lower the passenger side window; then I flung the waffle cone with the *vanilla* yogurt as far from the car as I could. I sat back in the seat and smiled over at him.

"Good idea, Nick, thanks." That made him angry. He was so angry that he pulled the car over to the side of the road and sat silently, his fists gripping the steering wheel for about five minutes. I looked straight ahead because I didn't have anything to say.

Suddenly, he started laughing. He laughed long enough for tears to start streaming down his face. I laughed, too, because the entire situation was ridiculous; especially because vanilla was my second favorite flavor. When he was able to control himself, he looked at me and took my hand in his.

"I don't know why I put up with your *crazy* ass. You are the most stubborn woman that I have ever met in my life." I started to protest, but he squeezed my hand just tight enough to keep me quiet.

"Look, Fiona, I get it. You're an independent woman. You ain't taking no shit and no vanilla yogurt from me." I smiled at that. "You don't like me half the time, and you're not letting your guard down for any longer than ten minutes. I believe you; you don't have to prove it every three or four days." He lifted my hand up to his mouth and kissed it.

"I'm sorry. I should have asked or told you about the yogurt. Now, can you just relax and let us get along?" I didn't say anything. I felt kinda warm inside, so I just picked up his vanilla shake and started sipping to cool myself. It was good. I couldn't stop the smile that spread across my face.

He took the shake back and told me that I owed him $3.86. He said he had children to feed and couldn't waste his money on a temperamental woman. I took a five from my purse and tossed it on the dash—my way of saying maybe I overreacted—and we shared the shake.

After that day we were more relaxed around one another. Nick was always pretty relaxed; it was me who changed. That day after he dropped me off, I did some soul-searching. I thought about what he had said. I remembered my vow not to turn into a bitter woman who was defined by a divorce.

I was a long way from being bitter, but I wasn't fully enjoying my life. Since my divorce, I had been spending way too much time subconsciously protecting something that was already fully protected . . . my heart.

The circumstances of my life had caused a barrier to be built around my heart that could not be penetrated by sweet talk and funny stories. I decided to stop acting like Nick could steal something from me if I let my guard down. So down went my guard, but the barrier around my heart remained firmly in place. And as far as I was concerned, that was a good thing.

CHAPTER 19

I was sick; so sick that I hadn't been into my office for two days. I wanted to rest, but I had so much work to do that I had to take my briefs to bed with me. Legal documents and Kleenex were scattered across my bed and my rug. Cold medicine, lukewarm orange juice, and cold chicken soup rested on my nightstand.

My mommy was on her way, and she was bringing me sweet and sour pig's feet. Mommies are good for that . . . taking care of you when you're sick . . . even when you're grown . . . *especially* when you don't have anybody else to do it.

I blew my nose and tossed the tissue in the general direction of the wastebasket near the nightstand; I missed. My mommy would probably clean up my room when she got here. I decided to push my work to the side and take a short nap before she arrived, but the phone rang and I picked it up automatically. I started coughing immediately after I said hello.

"Are you okay?" It was Nick. He hadn't been

over since I told him I was sick. Not that I *expected* him to come over, or that he was *obligated* to be concerned about me; I just feel like since he is a *chef,* you would think he would offer to cook me something. Hell, he could have *built* me something; he was always going on about his life as an architect. But it didn't matter to me because I had my mommy.

"I'm fine." My tone was dry.

"You don't sound fine. You sound like you have TB." I couldn't help my response.

"Then it's a good thing you haven't been over here; TB is very contagious." Nick laughed into the phone. He was always laughing . . . He made me sick.

"Are you mad at me, baby?" I had told him on several occasions not to call me baby.

"I'm not mad at you . . . for what? And I'm *not* your baby." I grabbed a tissue and blew my nose.

"I heard that, Fiona; that was gross." I blew my nose again harder.

"So, I'm sick, Nick, and sick people blow their noses, and *sometimes* when they blow their nose they get snot on their fingers." I know that my statement was childish and that I told you that Nick and I had a better understanding, but I was sick. It is not an uncommon thing for a man to offer to bring a woman some cough syrup or some tea when she's sick, especially when he's screwing her.

"My son will be here later. Do you want me to have him call you? He's at the age where he *likes* to talk about snot. He has some good fart jokes, too."

I smiled, but he would never know it. "Why are you calling me?"

"I know you're upset with me because I haven't been by. I left a couple of messages on your machine. I've wanted to get by there, but everything that could have gone wrong at the restaurant in the last few days has gone wrong." I had gotten his messages, but he hadn't known that I'd gotten his messages. I could have been dead or hospitalized for all he knew.

"Thank God for my mother, and my *true* friends," I muttered into the phone, just loud enough for him to hear me.

"Ouch. When I tell you everything that's been going on, you're going to feel worse than you do right now for being so hard on me. But listen, the situation here is under control, and I want to drop by and see you. Do you need anything?" Finally! But he was two days' late and a pot of "Fiona chicken soup" short.

"No, thanks. My mom is on her way."

"Your mom? I don't really believe that you have a mom." That was funny. Nick was always saying that I must have a terrible secret, because I won't let him meet my friends or my family or stop by my office. It was just me and him, and the strangers at whatever theater or restaurant or concert we went to most of the time. I interacted with his kids more than I thought was appropriate, but that was *his* doing. I kept the rest of *my* life separate, and therefore safe, from him.

"I do have a mother, it's just that she's a man-eating alien and I'm trying to protect you."

"Prove it and let me come over and meet her."

I sneezed three times. "Not today, Nick, I don't

feel up to it. Call me tonight before you leave the restaurant; I may need something then."

He sounded disappointed. "Okay, but if you need anything before then call me." We said our "bye-bye's" and I hung up.

I woke up to the sound of my mother cleaning my room. She had let herself in with the spare key and apparently had decided to leave me sleeping. "Mama, you don't have to do that," I protested as I sat up in bed. Of course, I didn't mean it. "Did you bring my food?"

She stopped her cleaning and sat on the side of the bed. "It's in the kitchen, baby." She held her hand to my forehead. "Have you taken anything for this fever?"

I nodded my head. "Just before I fell asleep." I was starving! My mother moved aside to let me get out of the bed.

"You need to wash your hands before you get into that food," she advised. I was walking toward the bathroom, but I turned to let her see the expression on my face.

"I know that I need to wash my hands." I brushed my teeth before washing my face *and* my hands. I walked into the kitchen wearing what I had been wearing for two days—panties and a thin T-shirt. For the record, I hadn't been wearing the same panties and T-shirt for two days.

My mom was in the kitchen dishing up the food. She had brought the requested pig's feet, vegetable soup, corn bread, and several humongous pieces of various desserts. I sat at the bar and waited, my stomach was churning with hunger. She put a bowl of vegetable soup and a piece of corn bread down in front of me.

"But I asked for the sweet and sour pig's feet, mom," I whined. I sounded like a teenager, but I tended to regress when I didn't feel well. My mother ignored my protest.

"They'll be in your freezer; pork is not going to make you feel better, this soup will." I didn't argue with her, I just put some of the soup in my mouth. My mother often forgot that I was an adult, even when I whined like a child. And as an adult, I could make the decision to eat the pork as soon as she left.

The soup was excellent. My mother's food was always so flavorful and fresh that I could enjoy it even though my taste buds were not in top form. I bit into her homemade buttermilk corn bread and closed my eyes to savor it. She always put a little honey butter on it before serving.

"This is good, Mom, thank you. What else did you bring?" I was talking at her back because she had started washing the few dishes in the sink.

"I brought some sweet-potato bread, some chocolate cake, some rum cake, some cookies, and a piece of pecan pie."

I was delighted and disgusted. "Ma, you know I can't eat all that stuff."

"Yes, you can. Good food makes you feel better. If you would eat better, then you wouldn't be in this situation." *What situation?* I had some kind of summer virus that had been circulating throughout my office.

"I can eat all that *sugar* and *fat*, but I can't eat a few little pieces of pig's feet? That doesn't make sense."

My mother looked over her shoulder at me and raised her eyebrow in warning. "It's not up to you to tell me what doesn't make sense. You don't eat pork when you're sick." My mother was stubborn.

"Then why did you bring it?"

"Because you asked for it, and you're going to eat it when you're well." I was going to eat it as soon as she left. I was about to continue my argument, but the doorbell chimed.

"Who is that?" my mom asked. I shrugged my shoulders and ate some more soup.

"It may be Nicole. She said she would stop by if she got a chance today."

My mother smiled. Nicole was like her third daughter. "Good, I have something to say to that girl." My mother left the kitchen to answer the door. I stayed at the bar and continued eating. She came back a few minutes later with a smirk on her face. "It's not Nicole. A *Nick* is here to see you. The hand that was about to put soup in my mouth froze for a second. My mom placed a bag of something on the counter and looked at me expectantly.

"Oh, he is." I tried to sound casual. The last thing I wanted was my mother asking me a thousand questions about Nick. "I can't believe he would stop by without calling. I'll have to talk to him about that." *I really would have to talk to him.* "Wait right here, mom; I'm going to put on a robe and go and see what he wants."

My mother snorted derisively. "Why?"

"Why what?" I asked.

"Why are you going to put on a robe? Hasn't he seen your naked ass before?" My mother laughed, pleased with herself for setting me up. I smiled tightly.

"Ha-ha. As a matter of fact he has seen my naked ass, but not in the middle of the afternoon." My mother looked at me doubtfully. "Well, not in the middle of the afternoon with my mother standing in the kitchen." I didn't wait for a response. I went through the side door of the kitchen back to my bedroom.

I put a beautiful black silk robe over my panties and T-shirt, then decided it was too sexy and changed into a white cotton waffle-textured robe. I brushed my hair into a smooth ponytail and checked the corners of my eyes for crusty uglies before walking into the living room to greet my uninvited guest.

Nick was *not* in the living room. I thought that maybe he had decided to leave, but then I heard laughter coming from the kitchen. *Shit! Nick and my mother were talking.* I turned toward the kitchen so fast I almost fell. I put a polite smile on my face and took a deep breath before walking through the swinging doors.

Nick was sitting in the stool that I had left warm, eating the *only* piece of pecan pie that my mom had brought for *me*. I was not happy. My mother looked up at me with the same smirk that she had had on her face when I went to put on my robe. "What's so funny?" I asked. My mother and Nick looked at each other and laughed again. I knew then that they had been talking about me.

"Nothing, sweetheart, Nick and I were just getting to know each other." I looked hard at my mother . . . She never called me sweetheart.

Nick took another bite of *my* pie before speaking. "Baby, you didn't tell me your mom is a champion baker." It was time to stare hard at Nick . . . I had told him a thousand times not to call me baby; I relented occasionally, but only when the lights were low. "Rita Mae, this is the best pecan pie I have ever had." My mother took the compliment in stride. She knew she could bake an old shoe, put her cream-cheese frosting on it, and start a fight over who would get the shoestrings.

"Thank you." Before I knew it, she was unwrapping the other treats that she had brought for me and placing them before Nick.

"Hey!" I protested as he was about to lay into my sweet-potato bread. "That's mine!"

My mother didn't look at me. She watched Nick's face as he continued to eat. "Fiona, you've been eating this stuff all your life, and half the time you complain about what it will do to your waistline. Don't you know how to let a man enjoy his food?" Nick looked at my mother approvingly. I stood in the middle of the kitchen sick and, I don't mind saying, a little sullen. Nick put his fork into my dessert over and over again (I mean that literally, not as some sort of sexual innuendo). My mother was staring at him like he was her firstborn son just back from a war.

I took the seat across from him and coughed pointedly. He looked at me closely.

"How are you feeling? You don't look too

good." I squinted my eyes in a way that did not improve my looks. "I brought some food from the restaurant that I thought you'd enjoy." His eyes were wide and innocent, but I knew that the only reason he had come to my home uninvited was to meet my mother.

"Thanks, maybe I'll just send it home with my mother. You two seem to have so much in common. She brought food for *me* to enjoy also." I put as much sarcasm in my voice as a stuffy nose would allow.

He puckered his lips and blew me an air kiss. "Don't be mean. I'm thinking of ordering some desserts from your mother to offer at the restaurant. I had to sample the products." My mother was a fast worker . . . less than fifteen minutes and she was about to close a business deal.

I listened as they discussed the benefits of using rum extract instead of the more popular vanilla in various desserts. They were boring and pissing the hell out of me. One of them needed to get the hell out of my house. I didn't care which one.

"If you two don't mind, I think I'll go back to bed. I'm sorry that I'm not in a position to entertain, but I need to take care of *myself* so that I can make it into my office tomorrow."

"Go ahead, sweetheart; I'll look in on you before we leave." My mother's look was challenging. She had warmed my pig's feet in the microwave and was insisting that Nick try them. He pushed his now-empty dessert plate aside and cut off a pig's knuckle with a clean fork. Nick closed his eyes in obvious pleasure. I could almost taste the sticky sweet and sour sauce.

"I have never had anything like this in my life! Do I taste ginger?"

My mother nodded her head proudly. "I'll give the recipe to Fiona for you." I didn't know what to do as Nick continued to eat and talk with my mother. I didn't want to leave the two of them alone together, so I just sat at the bar wiping my nose periodically as Nick finished the rest of my food.

"Thank you, Rita Mae. I'll go to bed happy tonight. The only home cooking I get is my own."

My mother shook her head sympathetically. "I tried to teach my girls how to cook. Fiona can cook, don't let her fool you. Young women today think the way to keep a man is sex. I been telling my girls since they left high school that a man can get a blow job for thirty-five dollars anywhere in the United States: it's hard to get a good homemade biscuit." See, that's exactly why I didn't want to leave them alone together!

"Mama!" I almost screamed at her . . . *almost* because I knew she wasn't above putting me in my place in front of Nick.

Nick laughed. "I never thought of it like that, Rita Mae, but you may be right. It's been a long time since a woman gave me a good biscuit." Nick looked at me and continued to laugh. Enough was enough!

"Nick, I don't mean to be rude, but I'm *really* not up for company right now. I'll walk you to the door." Nick and my mother said good-bye. He leaned down to hug her as if they were cousins. I was hardly able to keep my irritation in tact as I followed him to the front door.

"Your mom is a character," he said, still laughing. I didn't laugh with him. He responded to my negative body language by taking my hands in his. "You know I would have come by earlier, but it's been crazy as hell at the restaurant. And I know I haven't mentioned it, but I'm trying to buy another spot." That piqued my interest.

"Are you thinking about moving Nathaniel's?"

"No . . . It's something I've been dreaming about doing since my mom died." He let my hands go to look at his watch. "I have to get back to the restaurant now, but can I come by later so we can talk about it? I'd like to get your opinion."

Whenever a man starts asking for your opinion and starts wanting to talk to you about his dreams no good can come of it. Guard down . . . barrier up. I shook my head fast. "No, I don't think so." I didn't offer an excuse. Nick shook his head from side to side. I thought for a minute that I had hurt his feelings.

"You're a trip, Fiona. Listen to your mother, you may learn something." Then he turned and walked out without saying good-bye. I stuck my tongue out at the closed door. *Why I godda be a trip?*

My mother was waiting for me in the kitchen. "Nice man . . . good-looking, too. I don't know why you and your sister think you have to hide your boyfriends from us—"

"Nick is *not* my boyfriend," I interrupted her. "We're *friends.*"

"Call it what you want. You sneak around with your man, your sister sneaks around with her mystery man . . . you two keep all your "friends" a secret. Hell, if either of you died, we wouldn't know who to invite to your funeral." My mother was cleaning the bar as she chastised me. I knew that my mother wanted me to question her about my sister's "mystery man," so I didn't. I had other pressing concerns.

"I don't think it's proper etiquette to *invite* someone to a funeral. And speaking of etiquette, I also don't think it's appropriate to bring up blow jobs in a conversation with someone you've known for only fifteen minutes."

"Well, it's a good thing I don't have to concern myself with what you or anybody else thinks is appropriate." I scrunched my face up at my mother. She was a lost cause.

"Mom, I'm your baby girl and I'm sick. It would make me feel a lot better if for just once you would promise to at least *try* and watch what you say around my friends." Of course, she totally ignored my plea.

"There you go with that "friends" shit again. Fiona, if you've screwed him more than once, he's not your friend. And as good-looking and as fine as that man is . . . if you've screwed him once, you've screwed him twice." *God! How did I end up with a mother with such a fucking potty mouth?* I refused to lend credence to her statement by responding, but that didn't stop her.

"How long have you been seeing him? Is it serious?" I knew that if I didn't respond to her last question she would go home and tell my dad that I was engaged.

"Not very long," I sighed. "And it's not serious . . . It will never be serious." I hated it when my mother got that concerned look in her eyes.

"Why not?"

"Because, Mama . . . I know you don't believe me, but I'm through with all that. I'm not going through that man/woman drama anymore. The end result is always the same. It's not worth it." I was out of tissues so I went into the pantry for a roll of paper towels to take back to bed with me. The last thirty minutes had sapped what little energy I had. "You got lucky . . ." I told my mother as I ripped the plastic from the paper towels. "There aren't many men out there like Daddy." My mother's laughter surprised me.

"Baby, I know you love your daddy, and I love him, too. He's a good man. He doesn't drink, doesn't smoke, doesn't gamble; but at one time he was chasing pussy so hard I was scared he was gonna have a heart attack. And so there is no misunderstanding, the pussy he was chasing was not mine." I stared at my mother, speechless.

"You can close your mouth, honey, it's the truth. Your daddy and me have had a time in our marriage." An image of my father running with a baseball bat raised above his head chasing a heart-shaped vagina in high heels flashed before me.

"Mom, I've gone almost thirty years without that information. Why haven't you mentioned the fact that Daddy was a womanizer before, and why did you feel it necessary to tell me today?"

"Your daddy wasn't a womanizer, baby; as the kids say today, he was a *ho*. But to answer your question, I didn't tell you before because it's not your business. The only reason I'm telling you today is because as your mother I can't continue to allow you to mistake *bullshit* for *reality*.

"If you want to live the rest of your life alone, that's fine with me . . . as long as you're happy.

But don't do it because you think God stopped making good men in 1946. All it takes to make a good man is a strong woman. I didn't say anything when you up and left your husband, because that was your choice. You didn't have any kids to worry about. When a woman has children for a man, her whole life changes. If it wasn't for you and your sister, I wouldn't have stayed around trying to get your daddy to do right."

A coughing spell wracked my body, and her concern over my health prevented my mother from pulling out the soapbox that she always carried in her purse. I was grateful when she handed me a glass of water and insisted that I get back into bed before I caught pneumonia.

When she did leave, I lay in bed for a long time considering what she said about my father. I had always thought that he was the rock in our family—a hardworking man living with an eccentric and somewhat overbearing woman.

My mother had always been the unpredictable, moody one. How was I supposed to know that she had good reason to be moody?

I wanted what my mother said to be a lie; but I knew it wasn't. My mother didn't lie; she either told the truth or she didn't say anything.

As soon as I felt better, I knew that I was either going to have to reevaluate my *entire* girlhood or just tell myself that my mother's relationship with her husband was *not* my business. Just the thought of turning over the events of my childhood made me tired. I am not a person who likes to reevaluate things. I feel that it is a tremendous waste of time. Most of the time after I reevaluate a situation I come to the same conclusion.

CHAPTER 20

Go, Fiona, it's your birthday! It's your birthday! It's my birthday! I pulled into my parking space with a big grin on my face; it's not every day that a girl turns 30, especially one who looks 24 . . . *okay, 25.* I hummed the refrain from the parking garage, up the elevator, past the receptionist, and into my office.

I hung up the black jacket from my day to evening Armani pant suit before I plopped down into the soft leather chair behind my desk. The smile disappeared from my face when I picked up the brief I was working on. I was happy to give the birthday song a break. I tried, but I couldn't work up any enthusiasm.

Who was I kidding? I wasn't really that excited about turning 30. I'm not going to say that the first thing on my mind when I got out of bed was my ex-hole, and how he had promised me that we would be spending my thirtieth birthday making love on the balcony of some Parisian hotel. And I don't mean some Vegas hotel dressed up to look like Paris . . . I mean the *real* thing! I won't say *that*, but I *will* say fuck him and his empty promises.

Around lunchtime, just when I had forgotten that I was supposed to be in Paris, a posse of six burst into my office singing a different version of the birthday song. I pasted the grin back on my face and stood up to accept their well wishes and a beautiful bouquet of exotic flowers.

"Thank you." I smiled over and over again. I drew the line when they invited me to lunch. I told them that I had so much work to do that my plan was to work through lunch. My boss smiled approvingly, but I thought I detected resentfulness from some of the other well-wishers. My saying no meant that they wouldn't be enjoying a free lunch at a pricey restaurant.

"Do you have special plans this evening, Fiona?" my boss asked.

"Dinner with my family," I lied again. It occurred to me after I said it that no one in my family had called to wish me a happy birthday, not even my mother. I hadn't told Nick that it was my birthday, so we didn't have any plans. Even if I had mentioned to him that it was my birthday, our relationship was not such that I would *expect* something special.

I had to look down at my watch repeatedly before everyone got the hint and left my office. When the last of the bunch left, my phone rang.

Before I could utter my standard "Fiona Daniels here," my mother's less than melodious rendition of the birthday song assaulted my ears. "Happy birthday to you, happy birthday to you. Happy birthday to my baby . . . Happy birthday to you."

"Thank you, Mom; You too," I said distractedly.

"What do you mean me too? It's not my birthday."

"I know. I meant *thank you.*"

"I didn't have a chance to make you a cake this year. I'll try and get one in the oven before the weekend, but I can't promise. I've been so busy getting those desserts out for Nick. Did he tell you that it's been going very well?"

"We really don't talk about it, Mom." I sighed into the telephone. My mother had become one of Nick's vendors soon after their meeting at my house. I had protested of course; I'd told her that I felt uncomfortable with her working so closely with someone I was seeing. She basically told me that she didn't give a fuck. *She can make desserts for Nick's restaurant, but she can't make her own daughter a birthday cake.* "Is that why you called me, to ask me what I talk to Nick about?"

"No, crabby ass, I called to wish you a happy birthday." I don't know why, but her "crabby ass" comment kinda hurt my feelings.

"Well, it *is* lunchtime, Mother. Did you *just* remember that thirty years ago today you gave birth to a baby girl?"

My mother made an unpleasant noise. "I remember your birthday *every day*! That's what happens when you spend all day and half the night with your legs spread wide and on the verge of death trying to bring a new life into the world . . .

You spend a little time every day thinking about it."

Five points for the mommy! I had been duly put in my place. "You're right, Mom. I'm sorry. Thanks for calling."

"What are you doing tonight? Is Nick taking you out?"

"No, Nick is not taking me out. He doesn't know it's my birthday, and if you see him today, I would appreciate it if you didn't mention it to him."

"Why not? Are you going out with somebody else? I hope you're not cheating on him, Fiona Lisa; he's a good man, and you don't want to mess it up." I had explained to my mother repeatedly that Nick and I were friends, and that we dated casually.

"Mom, I'm not going out with someone else tonight, but if I did, I wouldn't be cheating on Nick. I'll probably watch a movie on cable, make myself some dinner, and go to sleep."

"I wouldn't do that if I were you, Fiona. They say how you spend your birthday is how you'll spend the rest of the year."

"I thought that was what they said about New Year's Eve."

My mother was always quick with a reply. "Well, honey, if you're alone on New Year's Eve, more than likely you'll be alone on your birthday. If you're not going to call Nick, why don't you call Nicole and your sister and have them take you out for drinks?"

I sighed again. "I may do that, Mom." Not! I knew that I wouldn't, considering neither one of those cows had called me to acknowledge my special day. I realized that my mother was the only person who gave a damn about me. I felt a sudden burst of love and affection for her. "Mom, why don't the two of us go out tonight and—"

My mother interrupted what was about to be a heartfelt invitation to dinner. "Shit! I think the timer on the oven is going off. Fiona, I'll have to call you back later." My mother hung up the line without saying good-bye. I stared at the receiver for a second before hanging up. I felt dejected and rejected.

I hadn't planned on working through the lunch hour, but that's exactly what I did. At about 2:15 my phone rang again. "Hello, gorgeous," Nick said before I could say anything.

"Speaking." He laughed and I smiled my first genuine smile that day.

"I heard it through the grapevine that today is your birthday. Happy birthday," he said warmly.

"I guess you spoke to my mother." She was always doing the exact opposite of what I asked her to do.

"My sources are confidential, so don't waste your time asking questions. I also heard that you don't have any plans for tonight."

"I do have plans. I plan to spend a quiet evening at home."

Nick made a disapproving sound. "Just like I said, no plans. Hang out with me tonight," he suggested. I thought briefly about my options. I could continue to insist that I had plans, or I could allow him to take me out for my birthday. I decided on the latter.

"Hang out where?" I asked with as much disinterest as I could manage.

"Let me worry about that. I'll come by your office and pick you up around four-thirty." Nick and I had been seeing each other for a while, but he had never been to my office and I wanted to keep it that way.

"No, just say where and I'll meet you."

Nick wasn't having it. "Fiona, I'm not going to have you driving all over town to meet me on your birthday. Be ready at four-thirty. I'm picking you up."

I continued to protest. "My truck is parked in the garage, I don't want to leave it."

"You are the most obstinate woman I've ever met. What's wrong? You afraid I'll run into one of your other boyfriends?"

"I don't have *any* boyfriends," I corrected him. "I'll have to get some things out of my truck before I leave, anyway, so I'll just meet you in the parking garage at four-thirty."

"If I didn't know better, I'd think you were ashamed of me." He tried to sound as if his feelings were hurt. I knew Nick well enough to know that his feelings weren't hurt, but even if they were . . . *so what!* It was bad enough that he and my mother had developed their *own* special relationship, and that his daughter had recently started calling my house for fashion advice, I wasn't about to be placed in a position where I would have to introduce him to my colleagues as "my friend Nick." The people I worked with asked questions for a *living*. I could hear them now . . . *So, how long have you two been dating? What does he do? Is it serious? Does he have a brother?* No thank you.

"Oh, I'm sorry I hurt the baby's feelings," I

mocked him. "Do you need directions to my office?"

"I know how to get there. I know where you work, when you work, how hard you work. I know a lot more about you than you think," he said with great confidence.

"Whatever, Nick. Just make sure you *know* how to show a girl a good time on her birthday."

"My sources tell me that you're thirty years old. A little long in the tooth to be calling yourself a girl, don't you think?" he teased. I ignored his question.

"Be in *the parking garage* at four-thirty and have something nice planned," I instructed.

"Oh, I think you'll be pleasantly surprised at what's in store for you."

When I hung up the phone, I felt a little better.

CHAPTER 21

Nick picked me up as instructed at 4:30. I opened the car door and got in like I had just robbed a bank and he was driving the getaway car. Nick was in no hurry to leave the parking garage. "Hello, gorgeous," he said softly, before placing an equally soft kiss on my lips. "Happy birthday." *Yeah yeah yeah.* I wanted him to leave the garage before anyone I knew came out of the building.

"If you exit on the south side of the garage, you won't run into as much traffic." I urged him to put the pedal to the metal. He leaned over and kissed me again, this time tracing my bottom lip with his tongue. I never knew how sensitive my lip line was until I met Nick. "Ummm." I forgot about the danger of being spotted for a minute and opened my mouth to let him know that I wanted to be kissed more fully.

"Happy birthday," he said again.

This time I acknowledged his birthday wish. "Thank you."

He put his car into gear and started out of the garage. "There's something in the backseat for you."

A big smile spread across my face, and I twisted around, stretching my seat belt to get the only shopping bag I saw there. Inside the bag was workout gear—shoes, a couple of sports bras, stretch cotton pants, socks, and a T-shirt. I don't know what I was expecting, but it certainly wasn't workout gear.

"Thanks, Nick, it's just what I wanted," I said with all the sarcasm I could muster. Nick laughed, as he often did at my sarcasm.

"I picked that up for you because I thought tonight would be a good night for us to start working out together."

I sat up straighter in my seat. "I work out already . . . religiously. I *know* you aren't implying that you have a problem with my body." I demanded an explanation.

Nick poked out his bottom lip and proceeded to mock me as I had mocked him earlier. "Is the baby mad? I know the baby works out." He placed a hand on my thigh and squeezed lightly. "Look how *hard* the baby's thigh is." I slapped his hand away.

"You are so stupid." I turned away from him and crossed my arms over my chest, then uncrossed them when I realized that I probably did look like a two-year-old. Nick laughed at me for a few seconds. When he saw that I wasn't amused, he stopped.

"I can't believe it, you're *really* upset." I turned to face the window when I felt tears sting the back of my eyes. I couldn't believe it either, but I was *really* upset. My thirtieth birthday was almost over and it had been one big fat disappointment. He placed his hand on my thigh again and attempted to console me as he maneuvered through the traffic.

"I know it's not the best birthday present, but I did just find out this afternoon that it's your birthday. I thought I'd get you a city-wide membership to the Y so that we could meet to work out together sometime. And I've been caught between your thighs enough to know that you are in excellent shape.

"I have a *great* night planned for you. We're going to work out, then I'm taking you by your place so you can change, and then we're going out."

It didn't sound very exciting to me, but he was right to remind me that he had just found out about my birthday. It wasn't his fault that I was feeling funky, nor was it his responsibility to ensure that my birthday went well."

"Thank you, Nick, that was very thoughtful of you. I don't know why I'm carrying my emotions on my sleeve. I guess that's what happens when you get older. I guess I'll be an emotional *basket case* if I live to be as old as you," I teased.

Nick lifted my hand and kissed it lightly. "Everything will be all right, Fiona."

Nick drove to a Y that was farther than I expected. When I commented on the distance, he told me that that particular Y had been recently refurbished and he worked out there whenever he had a little extra time.

Nick acted as if I had hired him to be my personal trainer. He told me what machines were the most effective and went to great lengths to explain the benefits of regular cardiovascular workouts. I already knew everything that he told me, but I kept my mouth shut.

After we both did forty-five minutes of cardio, he led me to the strength-training area. I had already incorporated weights into my workout, but I had to admit that Nick helped me take it to a different level. I was drenched and exhausted after another thirty minutes of lifting and stretching. "No more, Nick, I'm about to collapse." I protested after what seemed like a thousand sit-ups.

Nick agreed with me and extended his hand to pull me up from the bench. "I need a shower," I said as I wiped sweat from my forehead with a towel that the Y had provided.

"We both do," Nick agreed. He looked down at his watch. "We have enough time to take a shower and spend some time in the dry sauna."

I shook my head from side to side. "I can't shower here. I don't have a change of clothes, no soap, and no towels."

Nick started walking out of the workout area. "Yes, you do. There's two of everything in that bag, there's a body wash dispenser in the shower, and we can get any size towel you need at the front desk."

I shook my head again. "Let's just leave. We can shower at my place."

Nick sighed, then said with exaggerated patience, "Look, you need to take a shower, because we're not going to your place right away.

I'm taking you to this little boutique I know of so that you can pick out something special to wear tonight. I know the owner, she's pretty cool, but I'm sure she would prefer you to be nice and clean before trying on her clothes. *Damn*, but it's hard trying to surprise a stubborn woman."

A slow smile spread across my face. "Now, that's what I'm talkin' about! I like a man who's willing to take a girl shopping on her birthday! Nick, if you had said that earlier, you could have saved us both a whole lot of grief. Meet you by the front desk in thirty minutes." I kissed him lightly on the cheek as I scooted past him.

Fifteen minutes later, I walked out of the shower and into the sauna. I untucked my towel and arranged it carefully on the bench. I stretched out on the towel and let the dry heat envelop my body. Umm . . . Nick had been right to suggest the sauna. Taking a sauna was my favorite way to end a workout, but I rarely had time to indulge.

Just as I was about to fully relax, I heard the door open. I enjoyed being *alone* in the sauna. I sighed and started to sit up to make room in case the intruder wanted to sit on the top bench. I was about to wrap my towel around me when I heard Nick say from the door, "Don't cover up because of me . . . I've already seen it all." My mouth formed an "O" and my eyes widened as I stared at Nick in his gray shorts and white T-shirt.

"What are you doing in here? This is not a coed sauna." My voice was slightly raised, and Nick put a finger to his mouth to hush me.

"You're right, it's not, so I can't stay long." He looked me up and down as he moved to close the short distance between us. "God, you are so beautiful, Fiona." I forgot where we were for a minute and allowed him to take my face into his hands and kiss me. When his hands cupped my breasts I grabbed his wrists.

"Nick, are you *crazy*? You're going to get us thrown in jail. Anybody could come in here!" He hushed me again, this time by putting his lips against mine.

"I have a confession to make . . . The only reason I brought you here and suggested that we start working out together was so that I could get you naked in the sauna and have my way with you." He nibbled the side of my neck as he spoke. Nick took my hand and slid it into his shorts. As I have mentioned previously . . . Nick has a *nice* dick! I was scared, but at that point I was ready for anything.

"What if someone comes in?" I half moaned as Nick started to rain kisses down my shoulders and across my rib cage.

"Stand against the door and no one will be able to get in." I moved my body a few feet and leaned against the door. Nick followed, but knelt in front of me. "Are you ready for this?" He murmured the question against my warm thigh. He kneaded the back of my legs with his humongous hands. The heat was so thick in the small room that I could feel it resting on my shoulders. I listened to a droplet of water hiss to nothing on the hot rocks in the corner before answering.

"Listen, you need to know that if there's any trouble, I'm going to tell them that you raped me." Nick laughed and I sighed and leaned back farther against the door. I was ready. He moved his fingers in and around me before replacing them with the sure, strong, and languid strokes of his tongue. I curled my fingers in his hair and bit my lips to keep from making sounds that were sure to bring somebody running. The man was full of surprises.

Go, Fiona! It's your birthday. It's my birthday, it's . . . uumh . . . ooh . . . yes . . . oh shit . . . my birthday!

"You look outrageous in that dress." Nick looked me up and down and smiled approvingly just as he had done in his friend's boutique. I had tried on several dresses and everyone had agreed—and by *everyone* I mean myself, Nick, and the shop owner, Pasha—that the halter-style powder blue dress was perfect for me. It fell just below my knees, and Pasha had found sandals that were a perfect complement to the dress. She helped me with my hair and makeup, and when I walked out of the dressing room, Nick let out a long whistle.

"Why thank you, sir. I *feel* outrageous, and I assure you your generosity will be justly rewarded," I said in my best Southern Belle voice, which wasn't very good at all.

"I'll hold you to that promise, sweetheart." I didn't know if he was trying to sound like Groucho Marx or a perverted Clark Gable. And speaking of perverted . . .

"So you like to do nasty things in public places. I didn't realize you were such a freak." He looked at me and smiled.

"Well, apparently you don't know me as well as I know you. I've known you were a freak since I first laid eyes on you. And just for the record, I've never done that before, but you make me want to do things that I've never done."

"Oh, that's so sweet, Nick." Of course, I didn't believe it. "You're a man after my own coochie." Nick put his hand on my knee and tried to move it under my dress. He knew I wasn't wearing any panties. "Stop that." He complied and stopped the upward movement but let his hand rest on my thigh.

I looked at the scenery, then over at Nick. "Where are we going? It looks like we're pretty close to my house."

"We are," Nick said without explaining.

"Where are we going?" I asked again.

"We're stopping by your place so I can change. I have a change of clothes in my trunk."

"Well, why didn't you just change at the boutique?"

"Because I would like to brush my teeth before we eat for *obvious* reasons." I couldn't argue with that, so I sat back in my seat and relaxed for the rest of the ride.

Nick parked in one of the guest parking spaces at the condominium complex because my garage door opener was in my truck. His cell phone rang just as he was about to open his door. "Hello. Yes, honey, I told you earlier that I was taking Ms. Fiona out to dinner for her birthday. We're just pulling up to her house." He smiled at me and said, "Noelle says happy birthday."

"Tell her I said thanks." I smiled and was

about to open my door, but Nick held up the "just a minute" finger before directing his attention back to his daughter.

"She said thanks, honey. It's all taken care of. Sweetheart, I'll call you later okay. I love you." He ended his phone call, got out of the car, and then opened my door.

He took a garment bag out of the trunk of his car, and we walked toward my front door together. Nick tickled me from behind as I searched for my door key at the bottom of my purse. "Stop, boy!" I protested, but didn't really mean it. He slapped me lightly on the behind just as I pushed the door open.

I flipped on the lights and my ears were immediately assaulted by what sounded like a thousand voices shouting, "SURPRISE!" The first thing I saw when I recovered from the shock was my mother, my sister, and Nicole standing in the center of my living room holding a cake with what I presumed to be thirty lit candles. I looked back at Nick and saw that he had a huge grin on his face.

As they started to sing the "Happy Birthday to You" song, I looked around at the people assembled—my friends, my family, even my cousin Renee who I hadn't seen since she had gotten out of rehab for her sexual addiction, and the same coworkers who I had tried to avoid when Nick had picked me up that afternoon. All of them were standing in my house wishing me well.

I closed my eyes but didn't make a wish as I blew out the candles. I was overwhelmed, and when I opened my eyes, tears were running down my face. "How did you guys get this to-gether so quickly?" I asked to no one in particu-lar.

My mother answered, "Quick? It took us weeks to plan this party." When I looked around the room again, I realized that it must have. Two tables in the back of the room were covered with food—chilled shrimp and crab claws, fruit, bread, cheese, salads, there was even a small ice sculpture of the number 30 centered on one of the tables. Colorful gift bags were arranged on another table, and my furniture had been re-arranged to accommodate the more than fifty guests.

"I really thought everyone had forgotten," I said almost accusingly.

As she walked with Nicole to place my birth-day cake on the table, my sister called back to me, "We all know better than to forget *Fiona's* birthday." Now, if she had said the same thing two to three months before, it would have prob-ably led to an argument, but we had been get-ting along so well that I knew that the comment was just good-natured teasing.

"Well, I'm glad you know that," I teased back. I remembered Nick standing close behind me and decided the only thing for me to do was make some introductions. "Nick, this is my best friend, Nicole, and my sister, Ramona."

They all laughed and Nick said rather smugly, "We've met on several occasions, Fiona. Didn't you hear your mother say that we've been plan-ning this party for weeks?" The thought of Nick interacting with my friends and family made me more than a little uncomfortable, but I wasn't going to address it in the middle of my birthday party.

"Fiona, you look beautiful, honey. Sexy, but not like a whore," my mother whispered close to my ear as she gave me a birthday squeeze. Nick heard her and he laughed out loud.

"You have me to thank for that, Rita Mae, I chose the dress." I started to argue the point but he left and headed toward the bathroom with his clothes.

"Go look at what's simmering on the stove," my mother whispered again. It took me a while to reach the kitchen because my sister put a "pink panty" in my hand—a frothy cocktail made with pina-colada mix, rum, strawberries, and whipped cream—and I hugged and thanked many of my guests on the way.

When I reached the kitchen, my cocktail glass was empty and Nick was standing behind me. He had changed into dark blue slacks and a short-sleeved shirt that was suspiciously close to the color of my dress. "I know," he said. "We look like one of those couples who try to dress alike on special occasions. Believe me, I didn't plan *this.*" He gestured to our clothing. He didn't seem to be bothered by it, so I decided not to be either.

Before I lifted the lid from the large pot simmering on the stove I knew what it was. My mother had made my favorite sweet and sour pig's feet. I clapped my hands together in delight. Bowls and forks were placed on the counter along with a large slotted serving spoon. I picked up a bowl and served myself. My eyes closed automatically in pleasure after my first bite. "My mother has outdone herself," I said to Nick as I offered him a bite from my fork.

"Oh, Nick made that; he brought the pot over before he went to pick you up. All I did was give him my recipe." My mother had walked into the kitchen after us. I looked at Nick and the twinkle in his eyes confirmed my mother's words.

"You're just full of surprises, aren't you?"

"He is!" Nicole said. She and my sister had joined us in the kitchen. As my sister got ice out of the freezer, Nicole told me how the party came to be. "Your mother wanted to do something special for your birthday, and when Nick heard about it he practically took over. Well, *actually*, he did take over; he just told us what to do." Nicole went on to tell me that she and my sister made out the guest list and sent invitations, rearranged my furniture, and helped with the food. When she finished talking, I had tears in my eyes again.

"Oh my God! I love you guys." My mother, Nicole, and Ramona stopped what they were doing and all came around the island and caught me up in a group hug. I looked up at Nick but dropped my eyes before I could read his expression.

My party was in full swing, and after three pink panties, and two glasses of champagne, so was I. I had kicked off the beautiful sandals that Nick had bought me earlier and I was walking, *flitting actually*, around my house barefoot, eating, drinking, dancing, and socializing like the butterfly that I was that night.

Everyone at the party looked great. Ramona was obviously happy . . . she was glowing. I was hoping she would tell me something about her mystery man, but our relationship had not progressed to the point that we shared the intimate details of our love lives. But since she obviously knew who I was sleeping with, I naturally felt curious to know who was putting the smile on her face.

Nicole spent most of the night grinning up at her husband, Anderson. She looked beautiful, too, in white slacks and a lemon yellow halter top. She was wearing flats so she had to crane her neck back far to look at her 6'4" husband. I used to tease her in college about short women snatching up all the tall men from us tall girls who really needed them. *Stay with your own kind. I'm going to kick your ass if I see you with another man who's over 5'7,"* I would threaten her periodically.

My mother was flitting around the room also, and by the laughter and the shocked expressions that I saw on some of the faces of my colleagues, she was telling inappropriate stories as usual. My father was not there to rein her in, because according to my mother, his arthritis was bothering him.

I was standing alone nursing a third glass of champagne and watching everything and everyone around me when my cousin Renee approached me. "Girl, this party is off the chain." Renee watched a lot of music videos and she dressed and talked like it. She had on tap pants, some high heels, and a baby-tee with SPOILED spelled out across her breasts. "Is that your man?" She gestured to Nick, who was deep in conversation with Nicole and Anderson. *"He is fine as fuck!"* she proclaimed between clenched teeth.

I could tell by the look in her eyes that she was headed for a relapse. "He's not my man, Renee, but he is a *personal* friend." I looked at her pointedly when I said the word personal.

"So ya'll *are* fucking. Damn! I was sho' hoping I could get me some of dat."

She sighed with so much disappointment that I had to ask, "I'm not trying to get into your business, Renee, but didn't Aunt Sadie say something to my mother about how you shouldn't 'date' for several months." And by "date" she knew I meant go back to screwing anything and everything like she did before she went into "treatment." The small plate that Renee held in her hand was piled high with shrimp and cocktail sauce. She picked up one of the shrimp, dipped it in the sauce, and moved it in and out of her mouth. It looked to me as if she were giving the shrimp a blow job. Yeah, she was definitely about to relapse.

"They say I'm supposed to practice my breathing and occupy myself with things I love to do, but the problem is . . . I love to fuck." Renee looked down at the black leather watch that she wore on her wrist. "Girl, I have to go," she said abruptly. "Happy birthday." She leaned in and kissed me on the cheek. "Tell Aunt Rita I said bye, and if my mother calls you tomorrow, tell her I spent the night. Okay?" She didn't wait to see if I'd agreed to lie for her.

I shook my head as I watched her fly out of

the front door. Nick startled me by wrapping his arms around my waist from behind and burying his face in my neck. I looked around to see who was looking and everyone was. "Nick! People are staring at us." I tried to extricate myself from his embrace, but he pulled me closer.

"So. Do you care?"

"Yes, I do. My mother is here, and I work with a lot of these people."

He turned me around to face him, but not before sinking his teeth lightly into my neck. "You've danced with everyone here but me; it's my turn now." I laughed and pushed against his chest to get him away from me, but he held on tight with one arm and used his free hand to lift my chin so that I was looking directly into his eyes. "Why are you afraid to dance with me?" His gaze was so steady and so strong . . . and so *honest* that I couldn't think of a playful brush-off.

"I'm not," I said with more confidence than I felt. I don't know if he arranged it, or if it was just the universe working against me, but just as we started to dance my all-time favorite baby-making song was up on the CD changer. Whenever I heard "Reasons" by Earth, Wind & Fire on the radio I changed the station, because my response to it was so . . . *primal*.

"Reasons . . . the reasons that we hear. The reasons that we fear our feelings won't disappear." Nick moved me around the floor slowly and whispered/sang the words close to my ear. I forgot about how we looked to the other people in the room. The truth is, *and I know it sounds corny*, but I literally forgot that there were other people in the room. As far as I was concerned, it was me, Nick, and Earth, Wind & Fire.

Nick's arms were wrapped around my waist, and my arms were wrapped around his neck. I was on cloud nine. Tears slid down my cheeks, because I realized at that moment it was just where I wanted us to be. I wanted Nick to have his arms around me, and to touch my hair, and press his lips against my cheek, and dance me around my living room on my birthday. It felt so right, and I was afraid.

When the song was over, Nick held on to me for a second longer than necessary; then he tilted my head back and kissed me with all the steadiness and strength that I had seen in his eyes before our dance. "I'm so glad I met you, baby." He traced the tear tracks on my face with his thumb. We stood in the middle of the floor for a minute longer, and then my mother broke our trance.

"Ya'll need to take that to the bedroom," she said and thumped Nick on his shoulder. Everyone close enough to hear her laughed. Nick gave me a "we'll finish this later" look and released me with great reluctance.

My mother gave me a sly grin and grabbed Nick's arm. "Nick, my sister says she hasn't met you yet; come on and I'll introduce you."

"Save the last dance for me," Nick called back to me as my mother led him away. I found a wall to lean against as I watched them retreat. Suddenly, I wanted the party to be over.

Nicole approached me and I noticed that she

also had a sly grin on her face. "That was *some* kiss," she gushed. "Girrrl, you lucked out. Nick is really nice. I can see why you were so anxious to let him see your panties."

"*Girl*, get out of my face." Of course, she didn't.

"I'm serious, Fee! And he really likes you. And you like him, too . . . I can tell."

I neither confirmed nor denied her accusation; instead, I went in search of another pink panty.

A few hours later, all of the songs had been played, and most of my guests had gone. Mom and Nicole were cleaning up the kitchen, and Nick and Anderson were sitting on the sofa talking. My sister had left the party earlier, and from the look in her eyes when she left, I knew that she wasn't on her way home.

I was sitting on a chair all by myself enjoying one final glass of champagne, a satisfied smile on my face. Nicole and my mother came out of the kitchen, and I could tell they were about to leave. My mother was carrying a plate wrapped in foil. "Baby, I'm taking this food home to your daddy. I'll bring your plate back sometime next week."

"I took a couple of pieces of cake, too, Fee." Nicole held up the plate that she was holding. "Anderson, it's time for us to go home."

"Okay, babe," Anderson answered. I stood up and walked to the door with the rest of my guests. Nick followed Anderson from the couch and stood behind me like they were *our* guests.

My mom gave me a one-armed hug first, then she hugged Nick. Nicole hugged me also, but directed her parting comment to Nick.

"We did it, Nick. It was nice having you as a partner in crime. We should all get together sometime." Inside, I cringed, because I knew she was talking about doing the "couples thing."

"That's fine with me, as long as you promise to make some more of those pink pussies," Nick said warmly. We were all quiet for a second, then laughter filled the doorway.

"I believe they're called pink *panties*, Anderson corrected him with an enormous grin on his face. Nick chuckled at his Freudian slip, but I could feel his embarrassment. I refused to meet my mother's eye as I quickly pushed everyone out of the door. I could hear their soft laughter on the other side of the door as I closed it.

I turned to Nick with a look that was a cross between mortification and amusement. "I can't believe you said that!"

Nick shook his head. "I can't believe I said it either, but it's your fault."

"How is it *my* fault?" I asked immediately.

"Because when I'm around you, that's all I can think about. You look so beautiful in that dress, but all night I've been thinking about taking it off and making love to you." I walked into his arms and pressed my lips against his.

"Well, then, we'll have to do something about that."

"I have something for you," he muttered back against my lips. I slid my hands down to the front of his pants and squeezed.

"I know. I have something for you, too."

He pushed me away gently and looked at me. "No, not that . . . well, that *too*," he amended. "I have a gift for you in the garage. Go get out of that dress and meet me back here in eight minutes."

I looked over at the gift bags and boxes still unopened on the table and said something I thought I'd never say to a man again. "Nick, you've done too much already. I don't think I can accept anything else." And I meant it. All night Nick had been acting a little differently—intense, accommodating, and very affectionate. His attitude and *my* momentary lapse into la-la land during our dance earlier that evening was making me very uncomfortable.

"Go on, woman, and do what I told you to do."

I went into the bedroom, took off the dress as Nick had instructed, and tossed it across a chair. I took a short silk burgundy robe from my closet and a matching bra and panty set from my lingerie drawer. I slipped the robe on after I put on the sexy underwear. Nick's friend had arranged my hair in a very funky updo, so I took the pins from my hair and combed it out around my shoulders with my fingers. I looked sexy and wild . . . well, at least I thought so.

When I walked back into the living room, my jaw fell open. Nick was sitting back in one of the two Barcelona chairs that I had admired one Sunday afternoon at an estate sale to which he had taken me. The second chair was next to him. I had debated on whether to buy the classic chairs, but in the end had decided that the cost of restoring them would be prohibitive. And now they were in my living room and fully restored, courtesy of Nick Nathaniel.

"Oh, Nick, they're beautiful," I said as I stroked the black leather on the second chair and admired the simple lines. "It must have cost a small fortune."

"I have an upholsterer friend who specializes in this type of furniture. I bought the chairs, told him they were for a very special lady, and here they are. Are you happy?"

"This entire day has been incredible, Nick. Thank you. I am *very* happy."

"Well, come over here and show me," he invited softly. I got up and went to stand in front of him. Nick grabbed the silk belt of my robe and untied the simple knot. He placed his hands on my waist and kissed the skin right above my navel. I placed my hands on his shoulders to brace myself as he continued to make figure eights and circles on my stomach with his tongue.

"Did you like what I did to you in the sauna?" he asked.

"You know I liked it." I moaned my reply. "Did you like it?"

"I liked it so much that my dick gets hard just thinking about it."

I moved his hands from my waist and knelt in front of him. I unbuckled his pants and rubbed my hand across his white cotton shorts. "Is this for me, too?" He shrugged his shoulders and sat back more in the chair pretending not to care what I had in mind. I pulled his dick out of his shorts and stroked it, then blew on the head but wouldn't touch it with my mouth. "It's so smooth and so hard. What do you want me to do with it?" Nick shrugged his shoulders again but refused to speak.

I moistened my thumb with my tongue and ran it across the tip of his dick. Nick shifted in the chair and moaned. "Come on, Nick, I need some help. What do you want me to do?"

Nick stroked my shoulders and looked at me through hooded eyes. "I want you to put it in your mouth and suck it."

I nodded my head, and a slow smile spread across my face. "I thought so." He lifted his hips so I could slide his shorts and pants down his legs. Nick kicked the clothing across the floor and silently urged me to resume my position. I wanted to please him like he had pleased me earlier.

I used my mouth to pull on him, and I swirled my tongue across the head until it was moist and sticky. Nick buried his hands in my hair and pushed my face deeper into his lap. I knew he wanted me to finish the job, but I had other plans.

"Baby, don't play with me. Why are you stopping?" I could hear the frustration in his voice, but I ignored it. I stood up and slid off my panties. I held him steady while I slipped him inside me. We moved together better than we ever had. Nick moved his hips up and down, and I screwed my pelvis as close as I could get to his. It felt so good, so different, it felt like . . .

"*Oh shit!*" I tried to disconnect us, but Nick wrapped his arms around my back and held me down. "Nick, I didn't get a condom! Let me up!" I pleaded urgently.

"It's too late now, baby; just relax and feel this."

"No." I pushed against his chest, but he continued to hold me. He pushed himself deeper inside and started grinding his hips seductively.

"Nick, we can't do it like this; it's not safe." My protests were getting weaker, and I started moving my hips against him.

"You're safe with me, baby." He moved his face down to my chest and captured my breast between his lips. All my concerns melted and I gave myself over to the intense feelings that Nick was creating in me. He grabbed each side of my hips and moved my body up and down on his.

"You may be on top, Fee, but I'm always in control. Come on with me, baby . . . let go," he whispered against my lips. I did and he pushed us right where we needed to be.

Later, Nick and I were lying side by side in my bed. From the sound of his breathing, I figured that he was asleep. I couldn't sleep; my mind was racing because I was trying to remember the rules that I had set up for myself when I started going out with Nick. Apparently, I should have written them down and kept them in my panties, because though I couldn't remember *all* of "Fiona's Foolproof Formula," I was sure that having unprotected sex wasn't on the list.

I turned toward Nick and looked at his face in the darkness. The problem was that I had allowed myself to *like* him and to count on the time we spent together. Not good! One thing always led to another. If I didn't watch myself, I'd end up in the same situation that I promised myself I'd never be in again.

I pushed the covers back and was about to get out of bed when Nick grabbed my arm unexpectedly and pulled me back down. "Where are you going?" He sounded fully awake.

"I'm going to get some water. I thought you were sleep."

"I have too much on my mind to sleep." He sat up in bed and I sat up with him.

"Yeah, tell me about it. We acted like some stupid teenagers tonight. I can't believe we were so irresponsible."

Nick shook his head. "I'm not worried about that. If *you're* worried, I can take an HIV test and get you the results next week. I'm thinking about us." He took my hand in his and started tracing the lines in my palm with his thumb. "These past few months have been so good. You've added so much to my life—"

I cut him off midsentence, "That's just fuck talk, Nick."

"No, *it's not*, Fiona!" he said rather strongly. "Just listen before you dismiss what I have to say." He waited until he was sure that I was going to be quiet. "My feelings for you are very deep, and I think you feel the same for me, though I know you'll never admit it. I'm not asking you for anything. I just want you to know where I stand. I haven't been seeing anyone else since I met you, and I don't want to." He was looking at me, but I refused to meet his eyes. "Fiona, I just want you to know that as far as I'm concerned, you're my woman." He turned my face to his and kissed me softly on the lips.

"What does that mean, Nick? I told you when we met that I wasn't interested in anything serious, and here you are being all sentimental and shit." I was irritated. I wanted to kick him out of my bed, and I wanted to snuggle up with him and let everything go . . . I didn't have the strength to do either.

"I didn't want anything serious either, Fiona, but here I am . . . *serious*. I know you've been through a lot, and like I said, I'm not asking you for anything. I just wanted you to know what I feel." Then he laid back on his . . . *my* pillow and went to sleep, leaving me to consider his feelings and mine.

CHAPTER 22

I'm about to tell you the *whole* story . . . the rest of the story. The good news is that party was the highlight of my thirty years. Well, that is if I don't include graduating at the top of my class from law school, or my first *real* orgasm, or my wedding day. *My wedding day* . . . hard to believe . . . I know. But even though I married an ass, and therefore my married life ended quite logically in a big pile of shit, the day itself was quite spectacular.

My gown, my hair, the food, the music, and the feelings that I had that day . . . Everything on my wedding day was perfect. God, what a waste! But I digress . . . My thirtieth birthday party definitely made "Fiona's Top Five Memorable Moments" list.

The bad news is that soon, *very* soon after the party my circumstances took a downward turn. No, wait, that's an understatement. After the party, my life could only be described as *emotional hell on earth!*

I didn't speak to Nick directly about what he told me that night, but I started to do things a little differently. I guess I was testing the waters. I stopped cringing inside about the amount of time he and my mother spent trying out dessert recipes. When we were together with his kids, I allowed myself to relax. Nicole and Anderson came to dinner at the restaurant, and Nick and I joined them. I started telling him little tidbits about cases that I was working on. He would tell me about his plans to open up a sweet shop about three miles from Nathaniel's, and I would listen wholeheartedly. I would even venture to say that I was *supportive.*

Okay, don't laugh and don't say "I told you so," but I was kinda starting to think of him as a little bit . . . like he was my . . . you know . . . *boyfriend.*

I was doing very well at my firm. Clients were starting to ask for me, and my boss, Peter Hewleson, had started to take on sort of a mentoring role with me. He asked me to help out with some of our more long-term clients, and he invited me to dinners and luncheons where he wooed potential clients.

Peter—he asked me to call him Peter—arranged a luncheon meeting with some of the big wigs in the pork industry. If you know anything about Carolina, you know that pork is big business. Big business = lots of billing hours = big dollars for my firm. My boss arranged the when, my job was to arrange the where, and help him convince said bigwigs that our law firm was fully equipped to handle all of their legal issues, both foreign and domestic. I knew that the lunch was very important.

Since Nick was a man about town, I asked his advice about where the lunch meeting should take place. Of course, he suggested Nathaniel's, but he wasn't upset when I explained I preferred a setting where I was less likely to have sex in the back room.

He told me to take them to Minella's, an Italian restaurant with an extensive wine collection; a lush, quiet setting; and the best stuffed pork loin in all the Carolinas. He knew the owner and said that he would make sure we got VIP treatment from the time we stepped in the door.

I put on my Versace suit in preparation for the meeting, and also a money green silk shirt that Nick had given me . . . *just because.* I looked prosperous, professional, and sexy enough to warrant a warmer smile, but not so sexy as to distract our potential clients from the main purpose of our meeting. I'm not naive; I knew that my brains wasn't the *only* reason my boss wanted me along.

We rode in a gleaming Lincoln Town car to Minella's. And by "we" I meant my boss, *his boss,* and two middle-aged gentlemen from the PCNC—Pork Council of North Carolina. I sat between the two porkers in the backseat and made small talk with them during the drive to the restaurant.

I laughed politely at their pork industry jokes, and my smile didn't falter when one of them told me that the industry had always depended on the steady business of the African American community. I was a confident, cool, emerging young star on the Durham legal scene . . . and *da da da da da, I was lovin' it* (sung to the tune of McDonald's theme song).

There should have been a warning posted on the front door of Minella's:

DON'T GO IN THERE, GIRL!
or
FIONA DANIELS, ENTER AT YOUR OWN RISK!
or
SOYLENT GREEN IS PEOPLE!!

If you don't get the last one, that's okay. Unfortunately for me there was no note on the door.

The scene that I'm about to describe will stretch the limits of the imagination; it will stain the fabric of morality and decency; it will blow your naive little minds. *Ladies and gentlemen, welcome to the most pathetic fucking show on earth!*

The aforementioned party walked into the restaurant, *we* walked into the restaurant. I took charge and told the hostess that we had a table reserved. She looked on her little seating chart and her hazel eyes lit up. "Oh, yes, we've been expecting you." She said it like we were ambassadors from the United Nations. *Alright, Nick*! Her smile was warm and she was wearing slim-fitting slacks and a top that showed just a little too much cleavage for the afternoon. She took the right amount of leather-bound menus from the hostess stand and said with even greater warmth, "Follow me, please."

We were talking quietly on the way to our

table when I noticed something unusual, yet familiar, on the plush carpet—scales. Black and green scales made a trail from the entry of the main dining room to a table in the far back corner. I would recognize the scales *anywhere*. They belonged to my lizard snake ex-hole. Sure enough, my ex-hole was sitting with his back to the front entrance, his elbows were resting on the table, and it looked to me as if he was laughing at something.

Great! I thought to myself. *I have to eat where reptiles feed!* Fortunately, the hostess was leading us in the opposite direction. But just as we were about to turn, curiosity got the better of me, and I glanced again to see what form of human would join him for lunch.

When I saw the woman sitting at the table with him . . . holding his filthy claws . . . and salivating like he was full-flavor fat-free cheesecake . . . I stopped dead in my tracks. I couldn't believe it. My sister was holding hands with my ex-hole, and from the looks of things, it wasn't the first time.

"Fiona . . . Fiona?" I heard my boss calling my name and I heard the question in his voice, but I couldn't respond. I continued to stare at the monstrosity across the room. I stared hard until she felt it. Ramona turned her head just a little and saw me standing stock-still in the middle of the floor. The stupid grin froze on her face, then disappeared altogether.

My ex-hole turned to see what had caught Ramona's attention. When he saw me, he closed his eyes briefly and squeezed my sister's hand reassuringly. When he squeezed her hand I felt as if someone had started to turn the sharp screws that had been secretly planted in my aorta. The blood was draining painfully from my body.

I was a very rational person; lawyers by *nature* are rational people. So I knew I had a choice: one, I could ignore them, go on with my meeting, and deal with the situation later; or two, run screaming across the room and beat them both about the fucking head, no questions asked. *I choose to handle my business immediately!*

I left my party standing while I ran across the room screaming like a banshee. Somebody was going to die. Before my ex-hole could get out of his seat I pushed it back, and when he fell, I jumped on him and started pummeling his ass like I was Muslim and he was pork. I heard gasps around me, and I heard my Bitch-Sis screaming, "Oh, Fiona, I'm sorry, I'm so sorry!"

My ex-hole was trying to grab my hands, but I was too quick for him. I slapped him in the face so hard that *my* ears started to ring. I was glad . . . do you hear me? *Glad* when I saw blood trickle out of his nostril. You would think that he would have been able to push me off him, but he couldn't because I had superhuman strength. I was giving him the ass whooping that he had earned a long time ago.

"Please, Fiona . . . please," BitchSis whined. I slapped him one more time and turned my attention to her.

"Please, Fiona, *what*?" I screamed at her. "You ready for your ass whuppin' now?"

"If you don't leave right now, I'm calling the

police," the hostess threatened. "This is ridiculous." Her lip curled up in disgust.

"No, what's *ridiculous* is the way you have your titties hanging out. Nobody wants to see that shit when they're about to eat." She turned quickly, I assumed to go and call the police. I was going to leave, but I wasn't going to leave before BitchSis got what was coming to her.

My ex-hole must have sensed my determination, because he lifted his head from the floor and said, "Get out of here, Ramona." The concern in his voice added fuel to the fire in the pit of my stomach. I jumped up as quickly as I could and grabbed for the woman formerly known as my blood. She was quicker than I anticipated, and she grabbed her purse and ran toward the entrance of the resturant.

I looked at my boss standing near me with pity and embarrassment on his face. The pork fuckers were standing with their mouths open. "Give me the keys," I demanded.

"Fiona, that's enough." I turned back to where my ex-hole was still lying on the floor and kicked him in the balls. He groaned and the pain caused him to curl up and turn on his side.

I folded my body halfway to the floor and made like I was the Incredible Hulk. *"GIVE ME THE GODDAMN KEYS!"* My boss threw me the keys. I ran out of the resturant in hot pursuit of the evil betrayer, BitchSis.

CHAPTER 23

She was just getting into her car when I made it out to the parking lot. I ran to the Lincoln, pressed the button on the key, and got in. I was so incensed and so determined that she was going to get what was coming to her, I didn't fully close the door before I backed out of the parking space. The black door swung open and bumped the gray Mercedes that was parked next to me. From the sound of it, the door ding was substantial, but I didn't care.

I followed my sister closely through the streets. I thought briefly about running her off the road, but I wanted to kill her with my bare hands. She came to a stoplight and was forced to stop because the traffic was heavy. I stopped the Lincoln behind her and jumped out, leaving the car running.

My fists pounded hard on the driver's side window. "Open this door, you fucking slut!" I screamed at her. Sweat was running down my face. Two of the buttons had popped off of my money green silk shirt when I had been beating ex-hole. She glanced at me briefly, and her eyes pleaded with me to go away. She looked terrified. *"Open the Goddamn door, bitch!"* I screamed again.

I can truly say that I had no control over my actions at that moment. The light changed and she sped off through the intersection. The cars behind me started honking their horns immediately. Pedestrians walking along the tree-lined street had stopped to see what was going on. I jumped back in the Lincoln and continued to follow her. If she was smart, she'd drive straight to the nearest police station.

I followed BitchSis for about fifteen minutes more. I didn't pay attention to where we were going; I just knew that I couldn't lose her. When she pulled into a driveway, I was surprised to see that she had driven to my parents' house. My mother was standing on the front porch, so she must have called her from the car.

She jumped out of her car and ran into the house faster than I had ever seen her run. I turned off the car but left the keys in the ignition. I tried to jump out, too, but I tripped and fell on the concrete. I grabbed my knee and started screaming at the top of my lungs; it was a hard fall. My Versace pants were ruined, there was a long cut in the fabric across the knee, and I was *bleeding*! Now the bitch had cost me money.

My mother ran to my side. "Fiona, are you alright?"

"No, I'm not alright," I shouted at her as I struggled to get up. "But I will be!"

"Fiona, listen—"

I cut my mother off mid-sentence, "I need to talk to your daughter for just a few minutes, and then I'll listen to what you have to say. I limped toward the door, but I was determined to finish it. My mother ran in the house before me. I walked in the house and went straight into the dining room. It was where we had settled most of our family disputes when I was growing up.

My mother stood near the door with her hands held up and a look of determination on her face. "Fiona, this is going to stop right here."

"Do you know what she did? Do you know that she's screwing my husband?" I half cried, half screamed.

"He's not your husband anymore!" BitchSis cried from across the room. I tried to move toward her, but my mother moved in front of me. She made it obvious that in order to get to Ramona I would have to go through her.

"Did you hear what she just said?" I directed the question to my mother. When my mother didn't answer, I looked at my sister again. "You're supposed to be my sister! He should *always* be my husband to you!"

"You told me to go for what would make me happy. Well, *Wilson* makes me happy; I make him happy."

"Are you telling me that you were seeing him *then*?" I asked her incredulously. She didn't say anything, but the way her head dropped shamefully was response enough.

"Oh my God! You are so pathetic!" I closed my eyes against the rage that was boiling in me. My fists were clenched at my sides, and my breath was coming out in short puffs. "Well, your ass is gonna be sore when you're riding off into the sunset, because I'm going to kick it."

"Nobody is kicking anybody's ass around here. We can talk about this." I could tell that my mother was very upset, but under the circumstances I thought she was underreacting.

"Why do we need to talk about this Jerry Springer bullshit? She can keep having that motherfucker, but she's going to get her ass kicked first."

My mother gave me the mother eye. "Fiona, that's enough. Watch your mouth."

"Watch my mouth? You tell me to watch *my* mouth, but you uphold her in this bullshit? I can't believe it. How long have you known, Mama? Have they been over for dinner?" I asked sarcastically.

"Fiona, go home, honey. You're too upset to listen to anything right now."

I took a deep breath and said calmly, "I *am* going home Mama, but I told you I'm going to kick your daughter's ass." BitchSis spoke up, "What makes you think that I'm going to let you kick my ass? You *divorced* Wilson, remember? Fiona, why would you begrudge me this? We love each other." Tears and snot ran down her chin. She looked as if she expected me to answer her. The bitch was crazy, and I had had enough of the entire situation. My suit was ruined, I had probably lost my job, and BitchSis was screwing Ex-hole. I let out a long sigh; I was tired.

My mother took the sigh as a signal that I was ready to talk over the situation or that I was going to leave and go home. When I saw her body relax, I jumped on the dining table like the Bionic Woman and skated across to get to Ramona.

"Fiona!" my mother shrieked. "She's pregnant!" I looked back, stunned. I could see from the look in her eyes that she was telling the truth. Unfortunately, I didn't see that the table had come to an end. I took another step and fell to the floor. My leg crumpled beneath me. I screamed in pain. My mother ran around the table, and my sister approached me hesitantly.

I couldn't concentrate on anything except the physical pain that I was in. The heel on my shoe was broken. My mother and sister hovered over me, we were all crying for different reasons. After several minutes, I asked them to help me up. My sister took one arm and my mother took the other and lifted me from the floor.

My ankle wasn't the only thing that was hurt. I looked at both of them. My sister had chosen *dick* over *blood*, and my mother was standing by her. They had both betrayed me. I was through with both of them. I was determined to leave the house with as much dignity as I could muster. "Thank you," I said to my mother when I was sure I could stand up by myself.

I lifted my right hand and slapped Ramona across the face; then I slapped her with my left hand. She grabbed her face before I could see my handprint appear. I waited to see if she would retaliate . . . she didn't. It wouldn't have been a good idea for her to hit me back, not with her being *pregnant* and all. I walked out of the dining room and didn't look around when my mother pleadingly called my name.

The door to the Lincoln was open; I hobbled and slid behind the wheel. I started the car, but before I could put the car in reverse, a wave of emotion washed over me and I started crying . . . sobbing if you want the truth.

"Fiona, Fiona." I lifted my head from the steering wheel and looked at my mother. She had come out of the house to stand beside me in the car. I wiped my tears away on the back of my jacket, the suit was ruined anyway. "Ramona shouldn't have gotten involved with Wilson; she knows that as well as we do."

"How long have you known?" I asked her accusingly.

"Since last week. They came to me and told me that they were going to have a baby. Ramona was planning on telling you this weekend." The phrase "they were going to have a baby" made me gag.

"Why are you letting her hide behind you? Why don't you kick her ass out? Why are you even talking to her?" I was giving my mother a second chance to choose . . . and choose *me*.

"Because she's my daughter, too, and she's going to have a baby. The last thing a pregnant woman needs is unnecessary stress. As much as I disapprove, what's done is done. If that baby makes it into this world, and I'm praying that it does, it has to be your sister's *priority*. She and Wilson have to make a life for that baby."

"And you have to help them?" I asked sarcastically.

"Yes, I do, Fiona. I'm her mother; it's my job. When you have children, you'll understand."

"Could you move out of the way? I need to get out of here." My mother stepped aside, and I pulled the car door closed. I pretended that she wasn't there as I backed out of the driveway.

CHAPTER 24

I drove around for a while after leaving my mother's house. My ankle was throbbing, and on some level I knew I should go to see a doctor, or at the very least get home and elevate it, but I didn't. I was trying to convince myself that I didn't give a fuck about my ex-hole and the skeezer formally known as my sister.

I continued to drive aimlessly—or so I thought—until I found myself in the parking lot of Nathaniel's. Since I was there, I decided to go in and ask Nick to take me to the emergency room. My ankle had swollen to twice its normal size; I had already lost my favorite suit, I was not about to lose my foot over some bullshit.

I limped hopped to the entrance of the resturant. As I approached the hostess stand, Terri, the hostess, looked up. Her smile was warm for a split second, then an expression of horror crossed her face. "Oh my God! Fiona, what happened?" She left the hostess stand and walked hurriedly toward me. "Were you mugged? Are you hurt?"

Everyone at the resturant knew me, and I was embarrassed for her to see me in such a state. My suit was ripped and stained, my shirt was wrinkled and untucked, most of my hair had fallen out of the bun I had artfully created, my lipstick was smeared, and streaks of black mascara had dried on my cheeks. "I'm fine, I'm fine," I lied. "Is Nick here?"

"Yes, he's in his office," she offered distractedly as she continued to check me up and down. "Can I get you something, Fiona? Should I call the police?" I waved her concern away and walked past her on my way to Nick.

"I'm fine," I said quietly. I was aware of the glances that followed me as I walked through the resturant. Thank God I didn't have to walk through during the lunch or dinner crowd. One lady actually gasped and leaned into the man sitting next to her like I was going to attack her. I growled at her like I was a rabid animal as I walked past her.

I turned the corner. I felt better just seeing the door to Nick's office. I started smoothing my shirt before I realized how ridiculous that was. I knocked lightly on the door but turned the knob before I was told to come in.

The first thing I noticed when I pushed the door open were the oversized titties poised against Nick's ear. The second thing I noticed was the slender arm draped across his shoulder. The third thing I noticed before a blinding red color totally obscured my vision was the grin plastered across Nick's face. They were so engrossed in what they were doing that they didn't notice me standing in the doorway.

"Umh-uhm." I cleared my throat and leaned against the doorjamb. When Nick looked up and saw me, guilt flashed in his eyes before concern. He stood up quickly . . . or he *tried* to stand up quickly, but the hand draped across his shoulder impeded his movement.

"My God, Fiona! What happened to you?" His eyes were narrow . . . My eyes were narrow, too. The real physical pain that I was experiencing from my swollen ankle took a backseat to the crushing sensation that I felt in the center of my chest.

"Let's not talk about me, let's talk about your big-breasted friend here." I kept my eyes trained on her. Her expression said, "Oh no, she didn't!" My expression said, "Oh yes, I did, bitch!" Nick's expression said, "Oh shit!"

"Fiona, this is Sonja. Sonja, this is Fiona." His eyes pleaded with me or *warned* me not to cause a scene. I had no intention of causing a scene; I was in no shape to be involved in a second restaurant brawl. It was not my intention to cause a scene, but just as I resolved to keep my cool, it dawned on me that Nick had not qualified either relationship. One of the worst things a man can do to a woman, is not to make it clear in some way, shape, or form that he's fucking her.

That shit pissed me off, and the challenging look on Miss Titties' face did not help one little bit. She was wearing an intricate pair of three-inch sandals, something that a hooker would wear, only more expensive. The black lace skirt that she wore had a split on one side, and the lavender sweater would have been considered demure if not for all the breast flesh spilling over the top. Her hair was cut close and curled naturally just above her ears. In another situation I might have asked her where she found the peacock feather earrings that she was wearing, but there is a time and a place for everything.

"Sonja," I mused. "Is she the same Sonja that you were screwing when you were married to Yvonne?" Her eyes narrowed some more, and she stood up straighter. She looked like she was about to jump me or curse me out. I was ready for either. Her breasts were straining against the material of the sweater, and I was happy to see that one nipple was significantly lower than the other. Tacky tacky tacky! When wearing a form-fitting top, always, I repeat *always* make sure that your nipples are symmetrical.

"What the hell happened to you, Fiona? Were you assaulted? Mugged?"

"My sensibilities have been assaulted." I looked pointedly at the woman standing at the corner of his desk. Nick put his hand on my shoulder and I shook it off.

"Nick," Sonja said in a pseudocultured voice. "I'll leave these plans on your desk. I can see you're about to have your hands very full." She laughed casually as if my knowing that she was an adulterous whore didn't bother her.

Fake bitch, I thought.

"Excuse me? Who you callin' a bitch?" Either she was a mind reader or I had spoken out loud. I noticed her cultured tone had turned straight ghetto and her neck was rolling from side to side. It may come as no surprise, but I made an A+ in neck-rolling class.

"I didn't call you a bitch, I said you need to go check your saggy tit." That caused her mouth to fall open. Nick was looking at me like I was from another planet. You have to understand that my stress level was off the charts; I couldn't think straight because of the physical and emotional pain that I was experiencing. I would venture to say that I was in the middle of a temporary mini nervous breakdown.

Nick held up his hand to hold off the woman who was coming toward me. I didn't care. I was ready for another fight. "Sonja, I apologize, obviously something is going on. I'll get back to you as soon as possible."

"I don't need you to apologize for me, Nick."

Sonja looked me up and down and her expression made it clear that she found me lacking. "So this is Fiona? Good luck with that, Nick." She snorted and walked out after giving me one last pitying look.

"What the hell is wrong with you Fiona? Did you get hit in the head?" I forgot myself and put my foot on the floor. Pain shot up my leg immediately and I winced and would have crumpled if Nick hadn't caught me. "Forget it, I'm taking you to the emergency room."

"You're not taking me *anywhere!*" I screamed. "Where the fuck do you get off apologizing for me?" I didn't let him answer. "I come in here to talk to you and I find you holed up with some bitch that you used to fuck . . . could have just *finished* fucking for all I know . . . and you have the fucking nerve to apologize for *me*? You should be apologizing *to* me."

"You're being ridiculous, Fiona. Sonja and I were discussing *business.*"

"And what business would that be, Nick? The business of how far she could shove her big breast in your ear?" I could see that he was struggling to control his temper.

"You must have hit your head. You need medical attention. We can talk about this later, Fiona." He reached for me again and I took a step back. I bumped my heel against the wall and yelped again from pain.

"We don't need to talk about anything, Nick, but I *do* need to have my head examined. I can't believe I allowed myself to believe for one minute that your *I love you* bullshit could be true." He opened his mouth to speak, but I held up a warning finger. "And before you say *anything*, I saw the way you were looking at that woman. If I had waited another minute to make my presence known, you would have had her sprawled over your desk." To my mortification, I felt more tears streaming down my cheeks. My embarrassment only fueled my anger.

"Today, I found out that my sister is having my ex-husband's baby; but worse than that, I find out that despite all pretense to the contrary, you're just another fucking man, after all."

Nick stepped toward me again with a pitying look on his face. "Oh, baby, I'm so sorry." He tried to put his arm on my shoulder, but I pushed him back so hard that my good leg wouldn't support me and I fell forward as he fell back. I

heard a thump when the side of his head hit the
left corner of the desk and a loud clunk when
the back of his head hit the hardwood floor.
Thankfully, his chest cushioned my fall.

I grabbed the desk to support myself as I
struggled to my feet. Nick was lying still on the
floor. A small pool of blood was beginning to
form under his neck. The fact that he was probably dead registered instantly in my head. I was
horrified! I had not intended to kill Nick! As I
backed out of the room, I tried to remember
sentencing guidelines for involuntary man-
slaughter.

The hostess Terri and a couple of waiters were
hovering very close to the door. "Is everything
all right, Fiona? We heard some noise," she questioned anxiously.

"Nick is dead." I was surprised at my own
calmly uttered words. The three rushed past me
and into his office. I hobbled out of the resturant as quickly as I could.

My cell phone was ringing when I got back
into the car. It stopped after four or five rings,
then started ringing again almost instantly. I
lowered the window, snatched the phone, and
flung it on the side of the road. I wouldn't need
a cell phone in prison.

I sobbed hysterically all the way to my house.
I had decided that my only option was to turn
myself in to the authorities. My plan was to go
home, take a shower, call the police, and wait for
them to come and get me.

A silver blue Mercedes was parked in my driveway. It took me a minute to recognize that it was Anderson's. Nicole and Anderson jumped out of the car as I pulled into the driveway. I turned off the engine and put my head on the steering wheel, completely exhausted.

Nicole opened the door and tried to help me out of the car.

"I killed Nick. I killed Nick." I sobbed over and over again as she pulled me from behind the wheel.

"No, you didn't. He called me, and your mom called me. He said to tell you that some Terri was taking him to the emergency room for stitches. He said you were hurt."

Anderson grabbed one of my arms and Nicole grabbed the other, and they supported me as we walked up the driveway and to my front door. Nicole used the key that I had given her to open the door.

They placed me carefully on the couch. I looked at Nicole through sad tear-swollen eyes. "Did they tell you what happened?" I whispered.

"Your mom told me about Ramona and Wilson. Nick told me that you were . . . upset," she said delicately.

"Can you believe that shit?" I almost laughed.

"No, I can't." We looked at each other with sad eyes until Anderson interrupted us.

"Fiona, your ankle is broken. You need to go to the emergency room."

I shook my head from side to side. "It was broken earlier, but it's not anymore. It doesn't even hurt."

"That doesn't make any sense, Fiona. If it

doesn't hurt, it's because you're in shock. We need to set this ankle." I looked down at my foot disinterestedly. It was swollen to about three times its normal size. Anderson had taken my shoe and my knee-high off. My toenails were looking kinda blue under the clear polish.

"I'm not going anywhere. Can't you just cut it off?"

"Cut what off?" both Anderson and Nicole asked.

"My foot. I don't need it. I'm not going anywhere."

They looked at each other. Nicole sat down on the couch and lifted my head and settled it on her lap. "Baby, can't you set her ankle temporarily until we can get her to the hospital?" Nicole asked. "She's in no shape to go anywhere right now."

Anderson stood up. "I'll see what I have in my bag." He walked toward the door.

"And something for the pain, too, baby."

"I didn't know that doctors still carried bags around with them."

"Anderson does. He's always prepared for a car accident or a natural disaster." She laughed quietly as she continued to stroke my hair. "Everything is going to be alright, girl. Don't even worry about it." We sat in silence until Anderson came through the door with his medical bag. It wasn't black, it was navy blue.

He took out a small vial of clear liquid and a hypodermic needle. "This will help with the pain you're *not* feeling." He pulled a part of what was left of my green silk shirt off my shoulder and prepared the skin with an alcohol wipe. I looked as the needle pierced my skin, but I didn't feel it. I was completely numb.

It took the medicine less than thirty seconds to course through my body. I felt a wide grin spread across my face, then a silly laugh escaped me, and then I started to giggle. "What *is* that? Oh my God! Now I know why people do drugs!" As the medicine took hold, I felt a sensual feeling of complete well-being.

"It's morphine. It's probably a little strong for the type of pain you're experiencing, but it's all I had in my bag," he said apologetically. "She'll fall asleep before I finish setting her ankle."

Did he mean "she" as in *me* or "she" as in *her*, meaning Nicole? I wondered as I drifted off into a pleasant morphine-induced sleep.

CHAPTER 25

F our days later, I was sitting at my kitchen table. My broken ankle was elevated and enclosed in a purple cast. Nicole had chosen the color; she felt that purple was a better color to live with for six weeks than white. My mom and Nicole were sitting across from me. I was concentrating on wiggling my toes and trying hard not to listen to what they were saying. I heard the words "baby," "Ramona," "wedding," and I tried to cross my big toe over the toe next to it, but it wouldn't move.

"*Are you listening, Fiona?* I *said* nobody expects you to come to the wedding or be the baby's godmother, but you have to acknowledge what's going on. Now, I know this situation is hard, but that's just the way it is. You're a strong woman; this is not going to be the end of you." My mother's tone was firm but compassionate. I thought about breaking my other ankle so that Anderson would give me another shot of morphine.

Nicole reached across the table and placed

her hand over mine. She spoke quietly. "Fee, you have to talk about this." I jerked my hand from under hers and looked at my mother.

"Are *you* going to the wedding, Mother? Are you going to be the baby's grandmother? You're over here attempting some pseudointervention with me when your *other* daughter is marrying her *brother* for all intents and purposes." I was instantly pleased with myself; it was the first sarcastic remark I had made in over seventy-two hours. I was more pleased when I saw how my mother struggled to keep her sarcasm in check. Compassion only went so far with my mother.

"I've tried to explain to you that though I do not approve of your sister's choices, I am her mother and it is my job to support her through difficult times . . . particularly now that she's pregnant." I thought that was a pretty damned insensitive remark. I looked at her incredulously.

"I know that it's my job to support you, too, and believe me, I'm trying, Fiona. But you've always been stronger than Ramona. I'm afraid of what she'll do if she feels that I don't accept this situation." She was determined to piss me off.

"Mama, Ramona can die in childbirth. I don't give a fuck."

My mother stood up from the table and pushed her chair back. She thought it was the height of disrespect for children to curse in front of their parents. "That's enough Fiona!"

Nicole stood up, too, and put her hand lightly on my mother's shoulder. "Mrs. Daniels, will you make us a pot of coffee?" She stood without responding for a second before reluctantly walking to the cabinets. Ramona sat back down and sighed. She gave me a "you know your mama" look. She placed her hands over mine again and spoke so quietly that my mother would have to strain to hear her.

"I don't give a fuck about your sister either, but I do care about you." She didn't want my mother to hear her. I smiled because Nicole had always been a little afraid of my mother. She squeezed my hand encouragingly before starting to speak in a normal tone of voice.

"Fiona, everybody is worried about you. This is worse than before." Before was when I found out that my husband was cheating on me. "Your office is calling . . . You need to tell us what you want us to do with that car. You have cases you need to take care of. Fiona, you just can't drop out like this."

I cringed visibly at the mention of my office. There was no way that I could ever show my face there again. I could imagine the rumors that were circulating: "Fiona went crazy." "She's on drugs." "She attacked some innocent people in a resturant." "Did you hear she stole a rental car?" "She lost the company a very big client."

"Can you take the car back? I don't know where the keys are, but they have to be around here somewhere. And tell my boss I quit. Someone else can take over my cases," I said disinterestedly. My mother let the cabinet close a little too loudly.

"You can't just quit your job, Fiona. You've worked too hard."

"More than likely, I've already been fired." I resented them for involving me in this conversation.

"Well, you won't know until you talk to them. You need to return that car yourself." My mother couldn't concentrate on her task. Everything for coffee was on the counter, but she was looking at us. Nicole nodded her head slowly.

"I agree, Fiona, otherwise I would have already taken it back. But the car is not the big issue here. What's important is how you're going to deal with this situation. You almost went over the deep end, Fee, and if you don't come up with an emotional plan, I'm afraid you will." "Emotional plan" was a term that Nicole often used with her rehab clients. She was in deep social worker mode. "The way that you attacked Nick and hit him over the head like that. You haven't called him to apologize or to check on him—"

I interrupted her, "I *did not* hit Nick over the head! I keep telling you that he *fell!*" My voice was louder than I had intended it to be. My mother and Nicole looked at each other. "I don't owe him an apology. He's the one who lied to me." They looked at each other again.

"What did he lie to you about, Fiona?" my mother asked.

"Not that it's anybody's business but mine," I said to no one in particular, "but I walked in on Nick about to have sex with a woman that he committed adultery with when he was married."

My mother forgot about the coffee altogether and took her seat at the table. "Nick told me that you walked in when he was going over some design plans for his new dessert and coffee shop with Sonja, and you just went off." My mother said "Sonja" with too much familiarity.

"You know her?" I asked.

"I know *of* her. I know that she's an interior decorator, and that she's helping Nick lay out his new dessert and coffee shop. I know that Nick had to go to the emergency room, and that he has eleven stitches in the back of his head." She said the last part accusingly. Nick was her buddy. Ramona was her daughter. Wilson was her future son-in-law . . . again. She had to stand up and defend everybody but me. I took both my hands and lifted my injured leg and put it on the floor. I stood up and looked at my mother and Nicole.

"Thanks for stopping by, you guys, but I really need to get some stuff done around here. I'll figure out what to do about everything. . . . I always do. Mom, let me know where Ramona is registered." I wanted my voice to sound sarcastic and strong, but it sounded weak and hurt, just like I felt. Before I knew it, I was crying. My mother and Nicole looked at each other helplessly.

"Fiona, sit down," my mother instructed.

"I can't. I have some stuff to do," I said between sobs.

"Sit down," she said again more firmly. I plopped back in my chair, buried my face in the table, and crossed my hands over the back of my head.

"I don't love anything *more* than I love you, Fiona. I'm sorry if you think I'm being insensitive, but I don't know what to do either. I'm mad at Ramona, too, and I never did like Wilson." It sounded like my mother was crying and I had to lift my head to see. She was! My mother *never* cried.

"I would beat that girl's ass if I could. Everybody in the family is gonna find out about this shit, and I'm going to have to defend her, like I've defended both you girls all your lives. The bottom line is that Ramona is selfish, she's always *been* selfish, and selfish people tend to be alright.

"You like to pretend that you're all tough and that everything slides off your back, but I know it doesn't, Fiona. You have a right to be sad, angry, pissed off. This is not going to slide off your back, but don't let it stop you in your tracks either. You can't let this be something that you can't handle." Tears were streaming down my mother's face, and I was touched. "I've been so worried about you since you divorced. Pretending that you didn't care—"

Nicole interrupted her. Tears were running down *her* face. "Me too, Fiona. I've been worried about you, too. We just want you to listen to us and let us help you. Remember what I told you about listening to the people who love you. *We* love you, Fiona."

I sighed internally. They had come to console me, but I was going to have to console them. "I *know* you guys love me. I don't want you to be concerned about me. I had an *episode*, but as soon as I figure out what I should do, things will be fine. It's not like I've been a refugee from society for a long time. It's only been a few days." I got up and limped to the counter. I gave them each a paper towel to wipe their tears.

"I just found out some pretty devastating information . . . I need a minute. And, Mom, I *am* tired of pretending that things don't really get to me when they do. This hurts me, and I'm going to be hurt for a while, maybe forever . . . I don't know. But it's *not* the end of me." Relief was evident on both of their faces. "I'll take the car back tomorrow and see where things stand at my firm."

"What about Nick?" my mother and Nicole asked in unison.

"What *about* Nick?" I asked somewhat defensively.

They looked at each other briefly before Nicole spoke up. "Don't you think you should call him and straighten things out before too much time passes?" she suggested tentatively.

"No, Nicole, I don't. You didn't see what I saw in his office." I cut my eyes at her to let her know that it was time to drop the subject.

"I didn't see what you saw that day, but I did see how he looked at you the night of your party. I saw how much time and care he took to plan the party. I think he loves you, Fee. You shouldn't just throw that away."

I shook my head and held up my hand. "I don't want to hear it, Nicole." My mother held a soft fist close to her mouth as if at any second she would have to literally hold her tongue to keep from saying something.

"I'm just saying, Fee, you were very upset that day . . . Just consider giving Nick a chance to explain himself. Your perception *may have been* skewed."

I didn't say anything. I just hugged them both and thanked them for caring. When they left I went back to wiggling my toes.

CHAPTER 26

It took me another three days to drive the town car to my office. I got out of the car with a big sigh of relief. Driving a car with a broken ankle wasn't easy. I grabbed my crutch and hobbled to face the piper. I had knots in my stomach when I entered the building. I hadn't made an appointment to speak with my boss . . . I was half hoping he was out of the office.

Instead of the covert glances and forced smiles that I expected, I was greeted with genuine-looking smiles and concerned gestures. "Fiona, is your ankle strong enough for you to be putting weight on it?" "We were so worried about you." "I'll get you a cup of coffee." I figured they had all heard about my escapade and were afraid, *very afraid.*

"Are you going to be here for a while?" someone asked.

I shook my head. "I'm here to meet with Mr. Hewleson. Is he in?" I asked no one in particular.

"You want me to call Jermaine and find out?" no one in particular asked back. Jermaine was his assistant.

"That's okay. I guess I could just walk around the corner and find out." I walked past and felt several pairs of eyes staring at my back. Jermaine was sitting behind a maple desk in front of Mr. Hewleson's office. He was the perfect assistant for a partner in a major law firm—attractive, masculine yet oddly feminine, quiet spoken, and the epitome of professionalism.

"Fiona, great to see you! Are you here to see Mr. Hewleson?" he asked with great enthusiasm.

"Yes, is he available?" I answered with much less enthusiasm. He held up his index finger and lifted the phone.

"Mr. Hewleson, Fiona is here to see you. Yes, sir." He put the phone down. "Give him five minutes and he'll call for you. Please have a seat." He gestured for me to sit in one of the two chairs in the corner of the small room.

"If I sit down, I may not be able to get back up. I really shouldn't be on my feet as long as I have been." I leaned more on my crutch. A look of concern marred his smooth chocolate complexion.

"Oh, that's right. Your mom told us that you broke your ankle."

"My mom?" I asked incredulously.

"Yes, she was here yesterday. Beautiful lady. I was in the gym an extra hour last night trying to work off those chocolate chip cupcakes."

"My mom was here and she brought cupcakes?"

"Yes, didn't you know?" He seemed confused.

Just then Mr. Hewleson's voice sounded over the small speaker at his desk.

"Jermaine, send Fiona in."

"Yes, sir." I lifted my purse a little higher on my shoulder and took a deep breath before hobbling toward the big maple door in front of me.

He stood up and greeted me warmly. "Fiona, it's good to see you. I'm surprised. Your mother said that you wouldn't be in until sometime next week." *My mother again.*

"Well, I needed to bring the town car back." I was bobbing my head up and down slowly and I felt that the smile on my face was probably silly.

"Oh, yes, that's right. Well, are you going to need a ride back home?"

"Well, actually, my truck is still parked in the garage."

"Sit down . . . sit down." He gestured. This time I *did* sit down.

I had practiced what I was going to say in front of my bathroom mirror, but I couldn't remember anything. I decided to just go for it. "I'm sorry for everything that happened the other day, Peter. I apologize for the embarrassment that I caused you and the firm—"

He interrupted me. "Your mother has already explained the situation. In your circumstances I may have responded in the same way." I had to keep quiet, because there was no telling how my mother had explained the "situation."

"No one here knows what a great wrestler you are," he laughed, "except for myself and William." William was *his* boss. "He's willing to overlook the entire incident because the PCNC people loved you! They loved your passion and drive! They want you on their team. They said, and I quote, 'It takes a lady with balls to do what she did.'" I sat back in my chair . . . stunned.

"How's your ankle? Your mom told us you slipped getting out of the shower." Like I said, there was no telling what my mother had told everyone.

"It's healing, but I probably need to stay home for another couple of days."

He sighed. "I hate to be insensitive, but do you think since you're here you could take the PCNC file home with you? We'll be meeting with them again in less than two weeks to hammer out what we'll be doing for them."

"No problem." What else could I say? Peter looked at his watch and then at me apologetically.

"I was on my way out, Fiona. Jermaine will have those files for you." I stood up clumsily, still amazed at how things had worked out. "Fiona, tell your mother that her strawberry cream cheese cake was the best that I have ever tasted." *Chocolate chip cupcakes and strawberry cream cheese cake . . .* My mother had gone all out. "You'll have to let us know when that dessert shop is open." He got up and walked with me the short distance to the door.

"Jermaine, give Fiona the PCNC file, will you? Call me tomorrow, Fiona, after you've had a chance to look them over." I nodded my head . . . mute with my good luck.

"What did you tell my boss?" I demanded. My mother was taking muffins out of the oven. She calmly placed them on top of the stove before turning around to face me.

"I'm glad to see you're finally out of the house."

"What did you say to my boss?" I demanded again.

"I told him the truth . . . well, mostly the truth. I told him that your sister was involved with your ex-husband and you were caught off guard by it, and that what happened at the restaurant was an isolated incident, and that if at all possible he shouldn't hold it against you. Do you want a muffin?"

"No, I don't want a muffin. I don't know why you had to get involved. I'm a grown woman. Did you tell him that she was pregnant?"

"No, I didn't. I said what I had to say, left some treats for the people in your office, and I left."

I plopped myself down in a chair, folded my arms over my chest, and sighed. I had come for a fight, but I realized suddenly there was no need to fight. My mother had saved me the trouble and embarrassment of explaining my actions to my boss, and I still had a job.

"What kind of muffin is that?"

"Chocolate chip," my mother answered pleasantly.

"You have any chocolate milk?" She went to the refrigerator and took out a quart of chocolate milk. "No, I want white milk with chocolate syrup," I protested.

My mother shook her head. "Sorry, this is all I have."

"That's okay then."

She poured a glass of the milk anyway and

placed it and one of the muffins in front of me. She sat down and we stared at each other without blinking for what seemed like a long time.

"I'm sorry," she said.

"What for?" I asked.

"For the way I'm having to handle this situation."

I shrugged my shoulders. "I don't care. Do what you have to do."

"And you should do what you have to do, Fee."

I raised my eyebrow. "What is it that you think I have to do?"

She smiled slowly.

"Nick is about to open his dessert shop in another seven or eight weeks."

"Good for him," I said sarcastically.

"I have six dozen muffins that I need to get to the resturant for tomorrow."

"So." I took a bite from the center of the muffin.

"I want you to drop them off." *People in hell want to be in heaven.* My look was response enough. My mother sighed loudly.

"You have always been a stubborn girl. Let me tell you something, Fiona. You're hurt over one thing, but you're spreading it all over your life. When you think about your sister and Wilson . . . think about the truth. The truth is, your sister is a fool. She's about to marry a man who can't keep his dick in his pants; a man who doesn't have a problem screwing his ex-wife's sister. He's always had character issues . . . I knew that before *you* married him.

"Ramona loves him and she swears he loves

her, which is gonna add to her heartache when he shows her that he's the same Wilson that he's always been. When you start to feel bad about what Ramona did to you . . . think about the hurt that she's in for."

The thought of my sister getting what I thought she deserved—a life of heartache and misery—was extraordinarily comforting to me. I had thought of a thousand different ways that God could punish her . . . some so harsh that I would be ashamed to share them with anyone. But whenever I thought of her punishment, I thought of the alternative that filled me with fear and anger.

"But, Mama, what if they *do* love each other. What if they're really good for each other? What if Wilson changes into this wonderful husband and father, and they win the lottery, and have four more children, and Wilson becomes a Supreme Court Justice, and they live happily ever after?" I tried to make it sound like I wasn't really concerned about that possibility, but it had been keeping me up at night. What if they didn't get what they deserved? With hands that smelled like chocolate, my mother wiped tears from my face that I didn't realize were there.

"You know what, baby, everything that you just said could happen, but you can't worry over *their* happily ever after . . . You have to go and find your own."

CHAPTER 27

I walked into Nathaniel's with all the muffins my mama had given to me. Terri was standing behind the hostess stand just like she was during my last "visit." I could tell by the look in her eyes that she was a little frightened. "Fi . . . Fiona," she stuttered. "What are you doing here?" Her smile was forced.

"I don't think I have to have a *reason* to come here. I mean . . . it is a public eating establishment." I didn't smile at all. I hadn't done anything to her. I don't know why she was looking all *skerd*.

"No . . . it's just that . . . it's just that you haven't been here for a while, and the last time you left in such a hurry . . ." She let her sentence trail off. I held up the basket of muffins that my mother had given me and smiled brightly.

"My mom asked if I would drop these off."

She looked relieved. She held out her hands to take the basket from me. "Oh thanks, you can leave them with me."

I held the basket back and shook my head. "My mom said I should give them to Nick. Is he here?" *My mom, my mom.* I sounded like a Girl Scout. Before she could answer, there he stood. He had on a similar outfit to the first time I came in the resturant, the denim chef's coat with CHEF NICK embroidered across the chest, but he also had on a denim baseball cap.

"You here to finish me off, Fiona?" he asked casually. He stood close enough so that I could see the twinkle in his eye if he was teasing. There was no twinkle.

"My mom sent these over." I held the basket up higher. I sounded nervous even to my own ears.

"Yeah, I know; she called to warn me." He took the basket from me without asking and handed it to Terri. "Terri, take these to the back for me, please." She hesitated for a minute before taking the basket and moving toward the kitchen. Nick and I stood looking at each other. His look was disinterested expectancy; mine was awkward schoolgirl standing before the principal. When it became obvious to me that Nick wasn't going to, I was forced to break the silence.

"How are you doing?" I asked with a slight smile.

Nick touched the back of his cap. "Are you asking about the gash in the back of my head?"

"Not just that, but you know . . . things in general."

Nick looked slightly irritated. "Things in general are as you would expect. Is there something else, Fiona, because I have things to do around here?"

I could see that he was not going to make it easy for me. My eyes narrowed. I didn't like his attitude. My middle finger was itching. It was begging to be shot straight up between Nick's condescending brown eyes. But I remembered the sage words of my mother and decided to do something different and humble myself.

"Yeah, Nick. Could we go into your office for a minute? I need to talk to you," I asked demurely.

He looked at his watch, then back at me. "Five minutes."

Thanks a lot, I thought sarcastically. I had to clasp my hands together to stop my fingers from doing what came naturally. As I followed Nick to his office, I rehearsed the speech I had started in my car. I noticed a white gauzy bandage partially obscured by his baseball cap. I probably should have brought my crutch from the car to let him know that I was injured also.

Nick sat down when we walked into his office. I waited for an invitation to sit down also, but when I saw it wasn't coming I took the seat across from him. "Nick, I really need to apologize for my behavior the last time I was here."

"And by behavior do you mean walking into my office uninvited, degrading and cursing my colleague, assaulting me, and then leaving me for dead?"

I swallowed the protest that rose in my throat. "Yeah, that," I nodded. "I don't know if my mother mentioned it, but I had just found out some very devastating information. My sister and my ex-husband are getting married. She's pregnant."

"I heard." I thought I detected an itty bit of softness in his tone.

"I came here to talk to you about it, and when I saw that woman standing over you, it was like . . . another slap in the face; especially considering all the things you said to me." I couldn't help the accusation that crept into my voice.

"You were jealous," he said simply.

"No, Nick, I was hurt. I mean . . . after all those things you said to me . . . Why would you be seeing a woman who you had an affair with?"

"I'm not *seeing* her. She was doing a job for me. I *told* you that I had hired a decorator for the sweet shop."

"Yeah, you *did*, but you neglected to mention that the decorator was also the same woman who you had your illicit affair with!" I raised my voice to get my point across. "That wasn't right, Nick."

His voice was elevated when he spoke. "Is it right the way you've treated me all these months, Fiona? When I said 'all the things that I said to you' as you keep repeating, what did you say?"

"Actions speak louder than words, Nick!" I shouted.

"And what do your actions say, Fiona? That you can take me or leave me? That you'll break open my head before you give me the benefit of the doubt?"

I stood up clumsily and my middle finger had its way. "Fuck you, Nick! I said I was sorry." I turned around to get the hell out of his office, but he stood up, caught my arm, and turned me toward him.

"Look at you. You came here to ask me something. Instead of getting mad and running out of here like a damn drama queen, be a woman and do what you came to do," he challenged.

"I came here to apologize and I did."

"No, you didn't. You came in here to ask me what's going on between Sonja and me. You came in here to find out if I meant it when I said that I love you and I want you. You came here to see about us." Nick pressed his lips unexpectedly against mine for a brief second. "Are you going to leave, or are you going to do what you came to do?" He was right, that was what I had come for.

"Why are you working with that woman? And why was she all pressed against you like that?"

Nick led me to the sofa and sat down next to me before he started talking. "Because she's an excellent decorator, and she knows what I like. And before you say something sarcastic like "I bet she does," I mean in terms of aesthetics. There's nothing *sexual* going on between us."

"Nick, her titty was in your ear," I said doubtfully.

"Titty? Are you sure you went to Duke?" he laughed.

"I'm my mother's daughter . . . Don't try and change the subject."

"She was standing next to me because she was pointing out some details of her design plan. She *was* standing a little close," he finally admitted. "But I promise you it wasn't because we have something going on or because I wanted something to happen with her." I noticed that he said *I* and not *we*, but I didn't say anything.

"Her proposal was excellent by the way, but she's not the only decorator in the city and I won't be using her services for the sweet shop."

A smile started in my stomach, but I didn't let it reach my eyes. "Why not?" I asked quietly.

"Because I can see how that situation would cause you to be suspicious. Because I love you, and I want you, and I'm not going to let that be the reason that you back away from us. I want to do everything within reason to help you feel that it's safe to trust me." The smile moved to my eyes and spread across my lips. Nick covered them again with his own.

"If you love me and you want me, why haven't you called me and why were you being so shitty when I came in?"

"I didn't call you because your mother told me what was going on and I was trying to give you some time to sort things out about your sister and your ex. She told me that she would make sure that you called when you were ready. I am a little curious to know why you didn't call to check on me." He took off the denim cap and turned around so that I could see the back of his head. "I had to have the back of my head shaved and several stitches." I put my lips to the corner of his bandage in apology.

"I'm truly sorry, Nick. I didn't mean to push you so hard."

"But you *did* mean to push me?" He turned around and teased.

"I'm sorry . . . I was out of my mind." Tears

welled up in my eyes as they had so often in the past several days.

Nick pulled me into his arms and held me tight. "I'm sorry, baby. I hate that they hurt you like that."

The tears slid down my cheeks and I sobbed with relief. I was relieved to be where my instincts had told me to run to when I found out about my sister . . . in Nick's arms. I was relieved because right then and there I made the decision to stop being afraid and to give *love* a try.

When my sobs subsided, I looked at Nick. "My life has been better since I met you. When I think about it, I feel differently toward you than I did toward Wilson. I feel *more* for you."

"You love me."

"I love you," I agreed. "But what if some other woman comes along and stirs your interest and you decide to go for it? What if you hurt me?"

Nick stroked my hair and looked into my eyes. "I can't promise not to hurt you, Fiona. I don't know what next year or the next ten years will bring. But I can promise to treat you with love and respect . . . to cherish you and to deal with you honestly. Almost everything we do is a choice. Love is a choice . . . I choose to love you. I've learned from my mistakes what's important to me. I'm not a young boy, and my head is not easily turned. We both may get hurt in this, but I'm willing to risk it."

"What are you saying? Are you saying that if you cheat on me that it won't be because you don't love me, or that you'll be discreet or something?"

"No, Fee, I'm saying that I have no intention of cheating on you. That I want you and nobody else. That I will *always* be honest with you."

I looked at him for a *long time* before choosing to believe him. "Okay" was what I said. "But I *can't* marry you, Nick. I can't even think about getting married right now." I was surprised at his laughter.

"Woman, I didn't ask you to marry me. I haven't forgotten that you left me here to die last week. You have a lot of work to do before I would even consider asking you to marry me."

I was instantly offended and embarrassed. "Like what?" My head was cocked to one side and my eyebrow was raised.

"Like you need to deal with this situation with your sister, you need to deal with your ex-husband, you need to get your ass off your shoulder . . ."

"My ass off my shoulder? You've been hanging out with my mother too often," I said and rolled my eyes.

Nick ignored my interruption and continued, "You need to figure out if you're going to be able to trust me . . . *for real* . . . and to trust *yourself*. And then we'll see."

"Okay" was all I said.

EPILOGUE

That was the calm before the storm . . . or more accurately, the storm before the calm before the storm before the calm. Well, my sister and Wilson *did* get married, and she had her baby, a girl. They named her Mona Wilson; I know, when my Mom told me I reached for a bucket.

I don't want you to think that I'm gloating or anything, but the child is ugly. I haven't seen her in person, but I've studied the pictures that my mother has littered her house with and I can say with all objectivity that Wilson and Ramona produced a frightful-looking child.

I haven't spoken to my sister or Wilson, but I have thought a lot about their situation over the past several months, and I don't hold any grudges against them. One person's trash is another person's treasure. Don't get me wrong, I don't like them or what they stand for, but I may eventually take my niece out for ice cream. Humph . . .

with her looks, she's going to need all the positive attention that she can get *early* on.

Because of my remarkable handing of all cases given to me, I am now a junior partner at my firm, *thank you very much.* My mom has a job outside the home for the first time in her adult life. She is the lead baker/manager at Sweet's Nathaniel.

Nick and I are cool. So cool that I leased out my place four months ago and moved in with him at his invitation. He said, "I don't like it when you're not next to me at night." I said, "okay."

Oh, I almost forgot . . . Nicole is pregnant with triplets! Two boys and a girl. When that in vitro fertilization works, it really works! She has two more months to go and she's on complete bed rest.

I don't know . . . *correction* (as Nick is always saying) . . . I *do* know. I . . . am . . . so . . . happy and in love right now! This is the best time in my life! Nick can get under my skin like no man I've ever known, we fight a lot, but it's the good kind of fighting.

Nick does everything that he says he's going to do, he doesn't lie, and he makes me feel good. I trust him. Let me stop before I start crying. I really just wanted to share with you what I've learned about life in the past several months. It all boils down to this . . .

Fiona's Formula for a Fulfilling Future

Forgiveness

That's it! It has worked wonders for me. I know that I'm not the originator of that philosophy, but I feel like I am. I don't always remember, so I have it taped to the bathroom mirror. I'm not perfect; I'm just much improved. I don't have a lot of time because I'm busy busy, but I have something for you . . . go ahead and turn the page.

This little slip of paper should be hot in your hands.
It's the beginning of a love story:
His woman . . . her man.
He loves her and she loves him.
Their decision to make a life together is not a whim.

The sun will shine and angels will sing
Cause love unexpected is a beautiful thing.

On wings of love they will be carried.
Nick and Fiona are getting married.

Come and share your love and support for them.

New Hope Christian Church
June 10th
4 P.M.

Turn the page for a preview of
San Culberson's
IN BETWEEN MEN
Available now wherever books are sold!

At ten the following morning, Hope stepped off the treadmill and wiped the sweat from her forehead with the towel that she retrieved from the handle. Forty-five minutes ago the gym had been filled with people getting in an early morning workout. Now the circuit training area was almost deserted and Hope could use the weights without worrying about somebody wanting to "work in." She worked her upper body for twenty minutes before moving to her favorite ab machine.

Truth be known, she wasn't fond of *any* of the machines, but over the years she had made her peace with the ones that had proven to give her results she *was* fond of. She exhaled one last time, stood up, and wiped down the machine. At the *end* of a workout she always felt great.

Women in various stages of undress were positioned around the locker room. Hope took off her workout clothes and stood under the shower to rinse the sweat off before putting on her tank-style swimsuit. Today there was enough time in

her schedule for her to spend a few minutes relaxing in the sauna.

Waves of heat and steam greeted her when she
opened the door to the coed sauna. She found
an empty spot on one of the benches and sighed
as she sat down. Karl had called at around eight
that morning to make sure that they wouldn't
be picked up too early because "Aunt Stephanie"
had promised to make pancakes. She had assured
him that he would be there for the promised
pancake breakfast before hanging up. Going back
to sleep after that was impossible, so she put on
her gym clothes, got some post-workout clothes,
and left the house.

It had been an excellent decision to send the
kids away for the night. Ray and she had done
some memorable things the night before. Rarely
did she get the opportunity to spend time alone
with her husband. Their time together was mostly
family time . . . G-rated movies, school functions,
church . . . *When the kids are with his mom this
summer, maybe I can convince Ray that we should
spend a week alone on some tropical island. Yeah, right!*
She shook her head at the thought and leaned
back into the heat.

Her kids greeted her with hugs and kisses as
soon as she walked into the home of her best
friend. The two women had met at freshman
orientation at UT. They hit it off immediately
and had been pleased to discover that they were
assigned to the same dorm room. They continued to get along well, even though their back-
grounds were so different.

Stephanie's family was solidly middle class and had been for at least three generations. Her father was a dentist and her grandfather had been a mortician. Her parents had started saving for college before she started kindergarten. Hope had moved into the dorms almost straight from the projects and had qualified for all the financial aid that the state of Texas had to offer. After that first year, they had moved off campus to a nearby one-bedroom apartment and had continued to share an apartment until Hope and Ray had gotten married. Bad romances, academic probation, pregnancies, and life's many pitfalls had only strengthened their friendship. Hope had been the one to tell Stephanie that her mother had been killed in a car accident, and Stephanie had been in the hospital two and a half years ago when Hope's mother had taken her last breath. There wasn't much that they didn't share with one another.

After prying David's sticky hands from her bare legs, she sat down at the kitchen table and demanded coffee.

"I'm the one who's pregnant," Stephanie complained halfheartedly as she went to pour Hope a cupful. "You should be waiting on me. Help a big round sister out!"

"I am helping you out, girlfriend. You need the exercise." Hope blew out her cheeks and rubbed Stephanie's stomach as she placed the coffee in front of her. Her friend just smiled at her and sat down.

Stephanie was pregnant with her fourth child, and as with the other three pregnancies she had been exercising regularly and eating good, healthy foods. She was 5'3" and in very good shape. Stephanie and her husband, Lamar, had three boys also. Hope knew that most people thought the fourth pregnancy was a relentless effort on their part to add a girl to the mix, but the truth was they planned to have *at least* six children.

They believed that it was their responsibility as educated black folks to raise as many "bound to be successful" black children as they possibly could. In order to do that, they had foregone many luxuries they could have otherwise afforded. When it was time for them to purchase their home, they had searched for and found a modest house in a stable neighborhood. Stephanie had decided not to go back to work after their first child had been born. Five days a week and one Saturday a month Lamar drove the fifteen minutes to the dental practice that he shared with Stephanie's father. In the summer they took their children on special family vacations to broaden their outlooks and to supplement what they learned throughout the year. They lived modestly and saved almost every extra dollar for their children's education.

We could send a child to Harvard with all the money we spend on unnecessary things, Hope admitted to herself as she considered her friends' lifestyle. In reality she wasn't worried about the kids' school because she and Ray had a sound financial plan. Plus, she rarely made purchases that weren't budgeted . . . other than the occasional over-priced dress.

Toys were strewn all around Stephanie's kitchen, something Hope would not be able to tolerate in her own kitchen. *I'm not trying to be Ma*

Walton . . . and I did get my money's worth out of that dress last night.

"What are you smiling at?" Stephanie had a smile on her own face, ready to share her friend's amusement.

"Just thinking about last night." What part of last night would remain her secret.

"Did y'all have a good time?" Hope nodded and took a few minutes to give her the highlights of the party. "How was Lisa?" Stephanie knew of Hope's strong dislike of the other woman. Hope looked around the kitchen to make sure there were no children lurking in the background before responding.

"*Still* a bitch." She curled up her lips in distaste to illustrate her point. "If she didn't give such good parties, I wouldn't have anything to do with her." Stephanie laughed as she was supposed to, then got up to respond to a third call of *"Mommy!"* Hope drank the last of her coffee before getting up to join the fray in the back of the house.

They made it back home around lunchtime. Jordan, Karl, and David jumped out of the truck and ran over to their father, who was just finishing his weekly yardwork. Hope waved at her husband and went inside to start her own weekend chores.

Later, Ray suggested they spend the rest of the day in the backyard. He grilled hamburgers while the boys divided their time between the swimming pool and the jungle gym. Hope spent most of her time refereeing the frequent arguments that broke out between the boys, but she did manage to finish a few chapters in the book that she was reading in relative peace.

By early evening the boys were exhausted and their arguing was nonstop.

"*Mommy!* Jordan keeps splashing me and I told him to stop!" Karl shouting.

"But he splashed me first!" Jordan whining.

"First of all, stop that whining. Second, it's time to go in anyway. Get out of the pool and go start your baths." Mommy sighing.

"David." She raised her voice in order to get the attention of her younger son sitting in the sandbox. "It's time to go in." She knew David was tired when he got up without argument and started toward her.

"It's Saturday . . . Can we stay up late?" Karl again. Both boys were looking up at her like wet puppies. They were exhausted, but they would never admit it.

"I know it's Saturday, and you know tomorrow is Sunday. We're going to early service tomorrow."

"*Aww, man!* We never get to stay up late." Jordan this time. Tuning out the boy's complaints was a skill she had mastered years ago. Hope was determined not to be irritated by the fact that Ray wasn't at home to help with the boys. After the burgers were done and they had all eaten, he had decided to go to Oak Cliff to play basketball with some of his friends.

"Ray," she had said when he told her of his plans, "I thought we were going to spend the day together." He had given her his "don't start" look.

"We *did* spend the day together . . . and *now* I'm going to play basketball." Hope had started to say something, but she knew from experience that they would just end up arguing and Ray would *still* go to play basketball. So she had given him her "whatever" shrug and went back to reading her book.

And now I'm stuck here with three grumpy-ass boys.

Let it go, Hope; remember, you weren't going to let irritation get the best of you. The voice in her head was starting to be such a constant presence that Hope was thinking of giving her a name. She had considered "Screw that," since it was the phrase that usually came to her mind after the inner voice offered unsolicited advice.

"Please, Mommy! Please!" Hope was brought back to the present by the unrelenting whining of three little boys. They were following her through the house and pulling on her like little leeches. The patience had been officially sucked from her. She turned around suddenly and in her quietest, fiercest mommy voice . . .

"Jor-dan. Karllll. Da*vid*." Each name was pronounced with exaggerated distinction. "If you don't stop that whining *right now*, not only will you *not* get to stay up late, you will go to bed immediately after you take your baths. I said *no* and I mean *no!*" Then the boys made their way to their room without any additional comment. "Jordan and Karl, use the shower in the guest room and help your brother," she shouted after them.

As soon as they were out of sight she felt guilty. She hadn't shouted at them, but she had used a voice usually reserved for behavior more serious than simple whining and begging. She was not above apologizing to her children, especially when she knew they were not the root cause of her irritation.

The boys were busy getting their sleeping clothes together. Their fierce whispering stopped when they noticed their mother standing in the door. "Hey, guys." She smiled warmly at them to let them know that she had overreacted and that they were not in trouble. "If you hurry with your baths, we have time for some ice cream and a cartoon." She was rewarded with *"Yeahs!"* and big grins. Feeling a little better, she walked away. She loved her boys to death, and there was nothing that she wouldn't do to make them happy . . . *except* let them stay up late on a night when she was dead tired.

Three hours later the boys were fast asleep and Hope was freshly showered and fuming. Ray had been gone for five hours. She knew that the drive to Oak Cliff was fifty minutes round-trip from their house.

"They don't play four hours and ten minutes in the fucking NBA!" Hope muttered under her breath. She checked the clock again to make sure she was right about the time. She considered making herself a drink, but dismissed the idea immediately. Drinking to ease tension was the first step to becoming an alcoholic, in Hope's mind. Her thoughts then turned to the two gallons of ice cream in the freezer.

"And if I ate Häagen-Dazs every time Ray pulled some shit like this, I wouldn't be able to fit through the front door. And I won't give him the pleasure of having one more thing to complain about."

After the twins had been born, she had done

her share of raging at Ray. Complaining, or
"bitching," as he called it, that he needed to do
more . . . that he should be more considerate of
her needs . . . her feelings. Her mother had told
her that she just had the "baby blues" and that
they would pass. Hope hadn't argued with her
mother, but she knew what she had was the "I
just had these two babies and my husband ain't
doin' a damn thing to help blues." Her mother
had been right about them passing, though. Once
Hope had gotten it in her mind that her "bitching" wasn't going to do anything to change the
situation, and in fact, it seemed to make Ray more
resistant . . . she just stopped.

She had tried to focus instead on the positive
aspects of her life . . . she'd had *three* healthy
boys, a nice place to live, a good job, a man who
could tie her body in knots and with the swivel
of his hips have her feeling as loose as a goose.
She had decided to leave well enough alone. Ray
had been happy, grateful even, and Hope had
been *happier* . . . for a while . . . until she realized
that she hadn't *stopped* bitching, she just did all
of her bitching where Ray couldn't hear—*in her
head*. Her silence was more dangerous than her
complaining.

Hope shut down her brain as best she could.
She sat on the edge of the bed and massaged
her temples, trying to alleviate some of the pres-
sure that was continuing to build. By the time
she heard Ray pull into the garage she was lying
prone on the bed, covering her eyes with the
palms of her hands and fighting back tears of
frustration. She did some deep-breathing exer-
cises she had seen on TV.

Ray walked into the bedroom. Hope heard when he kicked his gym shoes off. She didn't get up from the bed . . . she couldn't get up.

"The kids asleep?" To her he sounded refreshed and full of energy. That pissed her off further. She fought to keep her voice under control.

"You know they're asleep, Ray." Her voice was tight. Still, she didn't change her position.

"What's wrong with you?" He had the nerve to sound really confused. *That's right, Ray*, she encouraged him silently, *walk in here all happy and pretend you don't know what's wrong*. She sat up on the bed and looked him straight in the eye.

"What's wrong with *me*, Ray, is that you leave a family barbecue that *you* suggested and don't come back for *five hours*. What the fuck is wrong with *you?*" Hope stood in front of Ray with her arms crossed over her breasts, waiting for an explanation. She hadn't meant for the profanity to slip out, but it had been right there on the tip of her tongue. Ray's face lost its pleasant, relaxed look and was suddenly scrunched up in anger. He hated it when she used profanity, especially on the rare occasions when it was directed at him.

"You *know* where I've been, Hope. I was gone a little longer because after the game we went back to Rodney's house to play cards. If you needed me for something, you should have called. You know I always have my cell phone with me." She took no pleasure in the fact that he hated explaining himself more than he hated her use of profanity.

And she *had* known all along how to reach him. She wasn't mad because she thought he had been out screwing or drugging or gambling or drinking . . . and she hadn't been on the verge of tears because she thought his car had crashed through a barricade on the freeway.

"I shouldn't *have* to call for you to come home, Ray. The fact that you were at Rodney's house is not important. What is important is that you think that after all these years you still have the freedom that you did when you were a teenager. Do you think it's right, Ray, that I spend my weekends caring for our children— and when I say 'our' I don't mean 'our' as in me and the fucking man next door, I mean 'ours' as in me and you—and you are free to come and go as you please. If you want to play basketball, you play basketball. If you want to go to the gym, you go to the gym. If you need to work late, you work late." At some point during their short conversation, Hope had decided to forego her no-bitching policy for good.

He didn't respond to her tirade. Instead he said, as though she was a lunatic that he was forced to live with, "You need to lower your voice before you wake the kids."

"If I wake the kids, I'll put them to sleep . . . like I do every night." But she did lower her voice. She didn't want the kids to be witness to their argument. It was really her argument, because as she spoke Ray was walking toward the bathroom.

"Hope, if you need some time for yourself, take it. If you were worried, I'm sorry. But I'm a grown man, and until that changes I will do whatever the hell I want." With that sarcastic bit he closed the bathroom door. And then there was nothing left for Hope to do but get in the bed. Her bitching had been as effective as it had been when she had given it up—not at all. But at least she had the satisfaction of knowing that he had been disturbed, if just briefly.

And she felt better. She smiled to herself when she recalled the look on his face when she had asked, "What the fuck is wrong with you?" *If I knock him in his fucking head I bet I'll get some respect and consideration around here.* Hope giggled aloud as she imagined the look on Ray's face if she got after him with the *famed* cast-iron skillet.

She got control of her glee and held perfectly still when Ray pulled back the covers on his side of the bed. He moved close to put a firm hand on her shoulder. His voice was warm and conciliatory as he spoke. "Hope, you know I don't mean to upset you. If you want to know where I am, call. If you need me to do something with the kids, you need to say so. I love you, baby. I don't like it when we argue." When she didn't respond, he started to stroke her back softly; he even went so far as to nibble her bare shoulder.

After a few more tries he sighed in frustration and turned his back to her. She knew that he wouldn't compromise his pride and *actually* beg. And if he knew her better he would know that she would not be swayed just because he approached her with soft words and a hard dick. Especially when she knew the only reason he was even attempting to apologize was his hard dick. Hope continued to take deep, quiet breaths until she fell asleep.